KEEPER

J. S. LENORE

Praise for
The Affinity Series

Books in *The Affinity Series*

KEEPER

February 2022

Published by Paranoid Shark Productions, LLC

Indianapolis, Indiana

This is a work of fiction. Names, characters, places, and incidents are the product of the author's imagination or are used fictitiously. Any resemblance to actual persons, living or dead, events, or locales is entirely coincidental.

ISBN-13: 978-1-7358445-4-1

affinityseries.net

To my readers

CONTENTS

CHAPTER ONE

T he only sounds in the hospital room are Cross's monitors beeping softly, the quiet rush of his breath, and the pounding of my own heart in my ears.

I don't look at my mentor, Taka, who's still standing in the doorway. I can't bring myself to meet his eyes, not with the anger simmering low in my gut.

Kim, Priya Sends. *Stay calm.*

I am calm.

Fighting down the stifling rage and betrayal, I ready myself for whatever Taka has to say.

"It started in 1979," he says, his voice low and soft as he begins but growing louder with each word. "I had moved from Tokyo to Chicago the year before, and I thought I was finally settled. I was working as a Burner. There weren't many of us here, and finding spirits to send on was easy. Lots of cemetery work, but not many *onryou* then"—he smiles briefly, the corners of his mouth high and tight—"though that changed as the years dragged on."

"Get to the point." The words burn my tongue.

Taka doesn't flinch, only nods. His acquiescence is

more unsettling than anything else he's done since walking into Cross's hospital room. "Of course. I met Ruth that year. She wasn't as successful then as she is now. We met at a neighborhood gathering, if you can believe it. I didn't know she was a Seer until later."

"That's a hell of a coincidence."

"You always were smarter than me." He smirks. "She knew who I was, knew how to find me. She's never told me explicitly, but I'm certain she Saw something. Maybe my name or face, maybe a date. Whatever it was, she and I met in 1979 and became friends." He swallows. "More than friends."

"Wait," I say, back straightening. "You and Ruth?"

"Not for a long time now, but yes, for a while."

Jesus.

"But that wasn't—*isn't*—important. She introduced me to a group. Other Mediums in Chicago. I didn't think it was anything at first, but then…"

"It was."

"Yes, though not for years. It was exactly what it seemed at the beginning. Mediums looking for community." He crosses his arms, his head hanging down for a moment before he looks back up at me. "You don't understand how it was back then. We were still seen as second-class citizens, Kim. The public distrusted us and our powers, even though it had been over a hundred years since we came out of the shadows. But prejudice is difficult to kill, and though it was dying, it was taking its time."

"So, what?" I want to stand, to storm around the room, but I stay seated and take Cross's hand in mine instead. "You had a social club. Did you sing 'Kumbaya' too?"

"You have plenty of reasons to be angry with me, Kim, but there's no need to be disrespectful."

The laugh rips itself from my chest. "You want to talk about disrespect? You've known this whole time what was happening. You knew what the marker was and what it was doing, and you kept it from me. I nearly *died*, Taka. One of those fucking ghosts nearly killed me, and you didn't think to tell me what the fuck was going on?"

His face is pale, but his expression is stony and still. "I did not know you were in danger. If I had, I would have told you sooner."

"So it only takes me nearly dying in a building collapse and some kind of Turned monster ghost to force you to tell me the truth." I can't look at him. "Great. Fucking fantastic. I'm real happy to know how you feel."

"Kim."

"No. Just…" I want to run my fingers through my hair, but I hold tight to Cross instead. "Keep talking."

"Those markers," he says, voice cracking. "I don't trust them or what Ruth is doing with them. But I didn't want to say anything while you were investigating. I thought… I hoped that you would find out more than I had been able to."

"And what were you able to find out from your ex?"

"Those Mediums she introduced me to, they were trying to direct the energy in Chicago. It was starting to pool in places, and wherever those places were, there were more ghosts Turning. We weren't sure, but we all believed that the two things were connected. Directing the energy... it was like building levies to prevent a flood."

Only now the banks are overflowing, Priya says, *and there's no way to stop it.*

"And what about my Affinities?" I ask, dropping fully into Second-Sight to watch the kaleidoscope of colors swirling around us. Blue-white, red, green, and now, golden yellow. The colors tangle around Taka's form, Claire standing behind him, her pale hand resting on his shoulder.

He lets out a shaky breath. "I don't know how that's happening, Kim."

"Bullshit."

His head snaps up, eyes flashing with barely repressed annoyance. "I mean it. I know I have betrayed your trust, but I am telling you the truth now. I have never heard of it happening before."

"Then why did one of your ghost pals know what was happening?"

His brow furrows. "What are you talking about?"

"At Oak Woods, at the marker there. The ghost who's guarding it said he had a second Affinity. He knew what it was like, what was happening to me."

Taka shakes his head, eyes wide. "I don't know what

you're talking about."

"Looks like you're not the only person keeping secrets, then."

Kim. Priya hovers between Taka and me, her mouth twisted in a frown. *I don't think he's lying.*

It doesn't matter. He's lied about enough.

"I know I should have spoken to you sooner, Kim," he says, his voice soft but firm. "It was a mistake to keep this from you, but I didn't think... I didn't realize how large the problem would become. I trusted Ruth—"

"More than me, you mean."

"No." He pauses. "Maybe."

His doubt hurts. I wish it were less painful, less of a repudiation of the many years between us. He's *Taka*, a man I've loved and looked up to for more than half my life. I don't want to hate him.

But I do right now, at least a little.

My anger leaves me in a rush, with only heavy grief left in the pit of my stomach. I miss the warmth.

"So, what's next?" I ask.

Taka scrubs a hand over his face, and it wipes away some of the dust that's still clinging to his skin. The streaks look like tear tracks through the grime. "I'll talk to Ruth."

"And you think she'll tell you the truth? All of it?"

"I won't give her a choice."

"Like you have before."

He looks away from me. "I'll find her. Now. Please,

send my regards to your… friend, once he wakes up."

I squeeze Cross's hand almost unconsciously, wishing he would squeeze back. "I will."

"I will see you later, Kim. And… I am sorry."

"Of course you are."

He nods once, then leaves, his shoulders bowed with a weight I wish I didn't understand.

"Fuck," I whisper into the quiet. "Fucking goddammit."

Priya's touch is cool and comforting, and I hate that I need it. But I still lean into it, my eyes closed against the prickle of tears.

I can't believe he's been lying to me this whole time.

He thought he was protecting you, Priya says. *I can understand that.*

I can't. I'm not a kid anymore.

You always see your kids as kids, Kim. You'll always be, at least a little bit, that eighteen-year-old girl who stood in the middle of my ruined home and asked me to help her.

I take a deep breath, pulling in air until my ribs ache, then let it go in a slow, hissed exhalation. *You think he still sees me as thirteen?*

Probably. He wants to keep you safe.

I can do that myself.

Priya huffs out a laugh. *You were just dragged out of the ruins of a building, Kim. And how long ago was it that you nearly got your ass handed to you by White?*

Shut up. She's trying to make me smile, and I'm not falling for it. *That's not the point. He knew something was happening to me and he didn't help.*

He doesn't know any more about what's happening to you than we do. So far, the only person who does know is dead.

I pull my feet into the chair with me, tucking them slightly underneath so my toes curl under the weight of my thighs. The unicorns on my socks smile back at me, cheerfully ignorant of the confused tangle of emotions building in my chest.

We need to go back to Oak Woods, I finally say. *We're going to have to make him talk.*

Priya's hand in my hair stills. *What are you suggesting?*

A binding.

Air hisses through her teeth as she breathes in. *He's not Turned.*

What other choice do we have? We need to know what's going on with me—I glance at Cross's placid, pallid face—*and what's happening to him.*

And you think Dave will have answers to that? Priya scoffs. *C'mon, Kim. There's got to be a better option.*

Give me one, and I'll take it. But he's our only lead right now. I lean back in the chair and close my eyes. *I don't know what else to do.*

The room's quiet again. The electronic echo of Cross's heartbeat is slow and steady, comforting. It beats in my chest as my power reaches for his. There's a hint of grass in the back of my throat, and the desperate desire to unleash the Healing energy, to pour it out of my body and into Cross's, sweeps through me. It's hard not to let it all come spilling out, not when the power and I both want the same thing. When I eventually give into the pull, it's a relief.

Carefully, I let a tendril of power free, and as I watch, it spreads from my fingers resting on top of his hand into his body, a weed finding its way through the cracks in the earth, hunting for a place to take root.

Careful, Priya says. *Hold it back.*

I nod, my muscles tense, and keep a tight rein on the power. The monotonous beat of the heart monitor picks up its pace, and a few moments later, there's a shuddering breath from the bed and my name carried on a whispered exhale.

"Hey," I say softly as I pull the energy back. "Glad you could join us."

"Fuck." Cross blinks at me, then slams his eyes shut. "Fuck. My head hurts."

"You knocked it pretty good when you passed out," I say. Sitting up in my chair, I lean forward and run my hand over his head. Another tendril of power slips free, sinking into his head. He lets out a grateful sigh.

"That feels so much better." He turns his hand beneath mine and tangles our fingers together. "Thanks."

Uncertainty quickly builds in my gut. "We've got a lot to talk about."

He makes a quiet noise of agreement, then turns his head on the pillow, looking at me with worried green eyes. "How are you feeling?"

"Tired," I say with heavy honesty. "You just missed

Taka. He says hi."

"I doubt that." Cross's brow furrows at the coldness in my tone. "What happened?"

I glance at the door and shake my head. "It's nothing."

"I know what you sound like when you're full of shit, Kim."

"I don't want to talk about it." My head pounds. "We've gone through enough in the last forty-eight hours. Just... let's take a breather, okay?"

His voice is hesitant when he says, "Okay."

Sitting in the quiet of his room, we don't speak. I keep running my fingers through his hair, watching as the brown strands slip through my grasp to fall across his forehead. Slowly, his eyes droop, then close. He falls asleep again, and I watch him rest, wondering how much he remembers of how things at the scene ended.

I remember everything, though. The way his power raced across the parking lot and covered the ghost in tainted gold, the way his eyes turned black and red, the pinprick of darkness still nestled in the center of his chest like the center of a bullet wound, charred dark and surrounded by blood.

I hope he can't see it. I wish I couldn't. I used to find comfort when I placed my hand over the symbol on his chest, but even though I desperately need comfort, need to touch him to know he's okay, I can't bear to place my fingers against the black smudge in the center of the mark.

Not now.

You should get some rest, Priya says, her hand on my shoulder a cool comfort. *You're still healing.*

I rub my eyes, pinching the bridge of my nose as I exhale. *I can't leave him.*

I can watch over him while you sleep. Priya floats to a low armchair in the corner of the room and hovers over it. *You'll at least be more comfortable sitting here than over there.*

She's not wrong. My lower back is aching, and though the Healing took care of the worst of the concussion, there's still a tightness in my shoulders that I can't stretch away. I let out another shaky exhale, squeeze Cross's hand one more time, and make my way to the chair.

Wake me up if he does, I say as I pull my legs up and sink into the cushioned seat. It's a bit too small, but as soon as my head settles on the back and my eyes close, I start to drift. *Or if anyone comes in.*

Just sleep, Kim. Priya's voice is hazy in my mind. *I've got you.*

Exhaustion sweeps me away a moment later.

CHAPTER TWO

W hile I've never been the best patient, Cross spends the next few days putting me to shame. I assumed he would want to be perfect for the doctors and nurses, following their every order like it was gospel. Instead, once the initial exhaustion wears off, he's antsy and anxious to leave as soon as possible.

"It's just," he says, his hands twisted in the thin hospital blankets, "I can't *do* anything while I'm in here. And I've got to do... something."

"You've got to rest," I remind him. "You're not going to heal from this overnight."

I don't say anything about the growing black stain in the center of his chest. It's worse than when he was admitted, though not by much. It looks like rot, like the darkness is eating away at the smooth, firm muscles of his chest with each inhale and exhale. Every time he runs his hands over it, rubbing against his breast bone as if soothing away an ache, I shiver and try to ignore the droplets of red that cling to his fingertips after.

That power slowly gathers in the room, too. There hadn't been a speck of it when Cross was first admitted, but now it's lingering in the corners and along the baseboards, a low hum of uncomfortable energy that makes my power gnash its teeth and pull at the tight control I have to keep over it. Priya and I share worried glances and do our best to keep Cross from noticing. He's still not used to Second-Sight, and I know he doesn't fall into it with the same familiarity and comfort I do. When he does and his vision goes distant, I stand between him and the energy, blocking it from his view as much as I can. I'm not sure if I'm effective at keeping him from seeing it or not, but he doesn't comment on it.

Thankfully, he spends most of his time in the hospital asleep or trying to find something to keep himself entertained. The first half of his thirty-six hours in observation are spent mindlessly flipping through TV shows, opening and closing app after app on his phone, and giving me puppy dog eyes when I refuse to sneak him out during the nurses' shift change.

I almost feel bad at the wave of relief that washes through me when visiting hours are over and I'm shooed out of his room.

"I can't believe you're leaving me in my hour of need," he says, mouth quirked into a grin that's only half rueful.

"You'll be fine." I take his hand and press a kiss to his knuckles, flushing as his teasing smile softens. "I've got your keys, and I'll be back with a change of clothes for you in the morning."

His green eyes are soft and pleading. "And coffee?"

"Christ, Riley."

"Please?"

Sighing, I kiss his forehead. "And coffee."

"Thanks, babe."

Eyebrows raised, I point at him. "Call me that again and there'll be spit in that coffee along with the cream."

He laughs and blows me a kiss as I flip him off before walking out the door.

Checking my phone as I head into the parking garage, I find a slew of missed calls from Andrea and a voice mail. Her usually calm, collected voice is rough with worry and anger.

"I swear to God, Kim, if you don't answer your fucking phone, I am going to find you and put you back in that goddamned rubble. Call me. Now."

My car starts sluggishly, and as I wait for it to warm up, I tap Andrea's name in my contacts list.

Priya settles into the passenger seat next to me. *This'll be good,* she Sends, eyebrow raised as she gets comfortable.

Andrea answers before I can respond. "Finally. Jesus." She sighs heavily. "What the actual fuck, Detective?"

"What... How do you expect me to respond to that?"

"I don't know. Why don't you start with what the hell is up with your partner?"

"Good question." I sink deeper into my seat, pushing it back so my legs can stretch out. I get the feeling we're going to be here a while. "His powers are…"

"Out of control. Like nothing I've seen before. Completely defying everything and anything I know about how Mediums work."

"That's a start."

"That's a start." She laughs, though there's not much humor in it. "How is our little atom bomb doing, by the way? He didn't look too good the last time I saw him."

"He's recovering."

"And what about…?"

I frown. "What about what?"

"The… *thing.* At the scene."

"The Turned ghost. Rivera."

"No," she sighs. "The one that possessed your boy toy."

I open my mouth to respond, but all I manage is a quiet puff of air.

"Kim? You still there?"

"Yeah."

"So, are we going to talk about it? It's a pretty big fucking deal that it happened, especially with all the fucking *power* that thing had."

"It's fine."

"Fine?"

"It's gone." I move the phone away from my mouth so she can't hear the ragged breath I take. "Cross is fine."

"Detective, as much as I appreciate what you're trying to do for him, lying to me isn't going to make the problem go away. If he's been possessed once, he's more likely to be possessed again, especially if that ghost is still lingering."

I think of the energy pouring out of Cross's chest, of the darkness staining his skin, of the way his eyes flashed red for a brief moment before he passed out on the pavement. Even with the car's heat turned on all the way up, I shiver.

"It's complicated."

Andrea laughs. "Yeah, no shit. What're we going to do about it?"

"So it's *we* now, huh?"

"I like the guy, what can I say?" Her joking tone shifts to something more serious. "We're going to do something to help him, yeah?"

"Yeah, of course." I rub my eyes. "I don't have any idea what that is, but yes, we'll help him."

"When's he getting out of the hospital?"

"Soon. They're holding him for observation, but I don't think he'll be there past tomorrow."

"Great. I need your address." There's rustling in the background and she pauses. "Or his, I guess. Wherever the two of you are going to end up."

"Andrea…"

"Don't *Andrea* me. Just tell me where to meet you so we can get this figured out."

"Fine." I rattle off my address, since I don't have

Cross's handy. "I'll text you once we get settled."

"I have a feeling," Andrea says, her voice distracted but clear, "it's got something to do with the symbol on his chest. It looks *exactly* like one I saw on those markers. No way his possession isn't related."

Swallowing against the sudden tightness in my throat, I murmur something like "What symbol?" and wince immediately.

"Really?" Her tone is flat, unamused. "You really want to go that route?"

"No," I force out. "We can talk about it later."

"Yeah. Take care of yourself, Detective. Your partner isn't the only one who needs rest."

"Will do."

"Talk to you *later*, then." She hangs up, and I let my phone fall into my lap. Staring at the screen until it winks off, I lean my head back against the seat and close my eyes.

Priya's been conspicuously silent, and I reach for her through our bond, hoping to find out how she's feeling. I'm surprised when I hit a wall between us. It feels as solid as brick, and whatever internal thoughts Priya is having, they're a complete mystery to me.

You okay? I ask before readjusting my seat and backing out. *It's not like you to shut me out.*

Priya glances at me, then out the window. *You're going to have to tell him what's going on.*

My gut twists.

You saw him, Kim. You saw the videos. What's happening to

him… It's putting other people in danger. It's literally eating away at him. You saw the mark.

I did.

So—she crosses her arms and leans against the door—*how long do you think you can keep this from him?*

I don't know how to answer her question. This whole situation is my fault. Riley wouldn't have that scarred symbol on his chest if it hadn't been for me dragging him to Elgin all those months back, if I'd stayed in his apartment instead of sneaking off into the night. Part of me wishes I could blame it on not knowing what I was getting into, but Baker was hardly my first Turned ghost. I should have been more cautious, more careful. Risking my life is one thing, but risking Riley's? My hands tighten on the steering wheel, and I stay silent as I turn onto the highway, pointed north, toward home.

Kim. Priya's touch is indistinct and gentle on my hand. I stare at her fingers resting on mine and take a shuddering breath.

I'll figure out a way to tell him, I say at last. *But let's get him out of the hospital first.*

Her fingers flex against mine and pull away. *Okay.* She sighs again. *It's not like we're short on problems. We've still got you and your powers to consider, too, and all of this damned energy all over the place.*

It's coming out of Death, I Send, my throat tight even though I'm not really speaking. *Through the tears.*

But why now? And why here?

I don't know. Maybe it has to do with the city or what Ruth's group is doing. Maybe they're fucking it all up.

Priya shakes her head. *They've been doing it for decades. Something changed recently.*

The catalyst is obvious, but I can't bring myself to voice that truth, not yet. My powers started changing after Cross's possession by Baker, after I Burnt his spirit with a symbol and my blood smeared across Cross's skin. He was Mundane before I put my bloodied hand on him, and now, he isn't.

It's so easy to think that Baker's the bad guy here, but in my heart of hearts, I know it's really me.

The car falls silent. Priya fades as the conversation dies. She's got to be tired after everything. Talking to Cross, stretching our bond so she could reach him, Healing me as much as she could while I lay trapped beneath tons of rubble with blood tacky on my face and my mind whirling and lost. I can't blame her for not wanting to manifest, but the sudden absence of her physical presence in the car leaves me feeling more alone than ever.

The road hums beneath my tires, and I find myself fading into the familiar emptiness of driving. It's enough to blunt the edge of panic from my mind, enough to let me distance myself from all the chaos of the last two days.

We get home faster than I expect. Somehow, traffic is light, even considering the time. I rumble into the parking lot of my apartment building right after the sun dips beneath the horizon, and as I turn off the engine and sit quietly for a moment, I have to fight the sudden feeling of déjà vu that rockets through me.

It's like I'm sitting in the shadow of the office building all over again. There's a man by the door of the apartment. His body is indistinct in the darkness, a shape that hints at stooped shoulders and graying hair. It's almost as if Cooper is waiting again, a lit cigarette dangling between his fingers.

Shaking myself free of the vision, I focus on the man and sigh when he steps into the light spilling from the entrance. He's just another tenant from my building, an older man I've seen a hundred times before in the elevator, the lobby, putting his trash into the chute. He's not Cooper at all.

My breath shudders from my lungs, and I hurry from the car, uncomfortable and tired to the bone.

The man waves at me as I walk past, and though I return the gesture, it's stilted and uncomfortable.

I'm too tired for this.

The trudge up the stairs to my floor seems like it takes forever, and the door sticks when I unlock it. I put my shoulder into it, sending it flying open with a bang. The sound echoes through the empty hallway behind me, and I wince. The last few days are catching up to me. My head aches with remembered pain.

Gently closing the door behind me, I slump against it and let my head fall back. With my eyes shut, it's a bit easier to breathe.

You should go to bed. Priya's voice is gently reproving.

I push myself away from the door and slowly amble my way to the bedroom. I'm still wearing the borrowed scrubs the nurses at the hospital foisted on me, and it's with a great sense of relief that I exchange them for a worn pair of boxer shorts and a tank top. When I slip between the sheets, my bed is cool, and as I fall back onto my pillow, Priya does me the favor of flipping the light off for me.

Thanks, I Send, already starting to drift.

For what?

The light. Even my mental voice is getting fuzzy.

I'm nearly unconscious, my mind swimming away on mindless thoughts that twist and turn into nothingness, when Priya speaks again.

I didn't turn off the light.

Still blurry and fighting against sleep, I force my eyes open. Falling into Second-Sight to find her in the room, I frown. *Yeah, you did. I didn't do it.*

I wasn't anywhere near the light.

But it's off.

Yes, Kim, I'm aware.

I roll onto my side. *I was in bed. I couldn't do it.*

Glancing at the wall, then back to Priya, I let myself fall deeper into Second-Sight.

Hidden among the blue-white, red, green, and gold is a thin, almost imperceptible strand of orange.

Ah, shit.

I'm wide awake now, and as I look around the room, I find more and more of the orange color twined with the rest. Tentatively, I reach for it, my hand outstretched even though my physical body has nothing to do with the power crackling through the room.

The light flips on, even though I'm feet away in bed and Priya is near the window.

Shit.

My fingers twitch, the switch flips, and the room falls back into darkness.

Shit, shit, shit.

Priya just sighs. *Looks like you've got another one.*

This is getting ridiculous, I grouse before falling back into bed and pulling the blankets up over my head. *And why couldn't it fucking show up while I was buried under rubble? It would've been fucking convenient then.*

You didn't have to get out of bed, Priya offers, as if that makes it better somehow.

None of this is better.

I don't want to be a Shaker.

Kim, Priya says with a bit of humor tinting the edges of her voice, *you're not a Shaker. I don't… Honestly, I've no idea what you are, but you aren't only a Shaker.*

A freak, then.

A unique and wonderful individual.

I feel her settle on the bed next to me, a coolness in the air that seeps through all of the blankets and the humid heat of my own breath trapped beneath the sheets.

I'd like to go back to just being me. Silence, still and echoing, grows in the space between us. Needing to break it, I let out a quiet sigh. *At least I didn't have to get out of bed.*

Go to sleep. Priya's voice is soft, and her touch on my face—her translucent fingers reaching through the blankets until they rest on my forehead—is softer. *Rest.*

She must push some kind of power through it, because a moment later I'm falling into sleep like I've been pushed off a cliff, unconsciousness engulfing me like the foaming waves of a deep, dark sea.

The morning hits me fast and hard. As the sun slants across my face, and I throw an arm across my eyes to try to shield them from the brilliant morning light, I groan.

Can't turn that off, I think before rolling onto my front and burying my face in the mattress.

Fuck.

It took months for me to start Reading, and only weeks since then to fly through Healer, then Speaker, and now Shaker. Seer and Passenger can't be far away, and though a large part of me wants to deny the possibility even exists, something in my gut can feel the other Affinities coming, like a train blaring through a tunnel, all light and sound until it smashes me against the tracks.

Falling into Second-Sight, I stare at the swirling mix of colors around me and sigh. Even without understanding how it's happening, I can't deny that it *is*. Better to face it head-on, right? I groan my way out of bed, brush my teeth, and look through my bookshelves for any introductory Medium books left over from college. There's one tucked behind an empty Kleenex box, the bright yellow USED sticker still wrapped around the spine.

What're you looking for? Priya asks, appearing over my shoulder to stare at the pages as I flip through the book.

Honestly? I stop when I reach the chapter on Shakers. *Anything at all at this point. I mean, there's got to be something, right?*

It's basic, but it's better than nothing, she agrees. *Might as well start practicing.*

I skim through the exercises listed in the book, as well as some of the theory behind Shakers and how their powers work. As I wait for my coffee to brew, I grab a penny from my junk drawer and set it on the table. I focus on it, reaching with the new power flickering around me in Second-Sight, and give it a gentle push across the counter. Though it only moves a few inches, sweat gathers between my shoulder blades.

That's harder than it looks, I Send as I let go of the coin.

Priya touches her finger to it, then pushes the tip through the metal. *I bet. Metal's hard to move.*

The light switch is plastic. Might be why it was so easy.

Opening the fridge, I twist the lid off a half gallon of milk and set it down on the counter next to the penny. A moment later, I reach out with my power and give the cap a push. It skitters across the surface easily, tapping against the backsplash with enough force to flip over.

Interesting. Great party trick, but I don't think I'll be doing much more than that.

Priya hums softly, her lip caught between her teeth as she thinks. *Maybe. Your other Affinities came on slow to start with, then grew more powerful. Give it time.*

As if time is something we have an overabundance of. I try to keep the irritation from building and take a deep breath, hold it, and let it go slowly. The coffee maker beeps helpfully, and I pour myself a cup while Priya idly flips through the book.

I take a careful sip, considering. *Do you think...?* I start before cutting myself off.

Think what?

Dave said that he got a second Affinity. Do you think there are others? Mediums with more than one Affinity?

Others like you?

I shrug. *Maybe. I don't know.*

I think, she Sends before settling next to me on the counter, *that there's a possibility there might be others like you, yes. Other Mediums with more than one Affinity. But—*her voice is gentle, though I flinch at the word—*I would be surprised if there were any other Mediums with as many Affinities as you. I don't exactly think it's going to stop with Shaker, Kim. Not with how quickly they've been coming and how powerful you've become.*

I hide my face in my cup. Closing my eyes, I breathe in the familiar smell of dark roast and try to pretend like we're back before Baker, before any of this started. For a brief second, I'm able to hold on to that feeling and sink into the comfort of not worrying about what's happening to me or to Cross or to Chicago.

Something metallic falls to the floor, and when I open my eyes, the penny rests between my feet on the kitchen tile.

So much for that.

C'mon, I Send as I finish the last swallow of coffee. *We should get over to the hospital.*

Chapter Three

P riya and I sneak into the hospital before visiting hours to see Cross the next morning, bribing my way past the nurses' station with coffee and doughnuts. I recognize a few of them from the shift the night before, and at least one of the nurses gives me a commiserating smile as I pass her a cup of coffee from the drink carrier I'm holding.

"Thank you for this. The stuff from the cafeteria is awful." She takes a grateful sip and lets out a contented sigh. "Your partner's been resting fine all night. Perfectly well-behaved."

"Is he up?"

"As of twenty minutes ago. Go on in. I'm sure he'll be happy to see you."

Smiling my thanks, I head down the hall toward Cross's room and walk past a few nurses I didn't see the night before. They're leaning in close together and talking quietly, mouths quirked in mischievous grins.

"Did you see the guy in 13F?" one of them says conspiratorially.

The other nurse laughs. "Did I? I nearly took his blood pressure a second time just to stay longer."

13F is Cross's room, and as the pair of women walk past me, laughing together, jealousy twists in my stomach. I shove it down, embarrassed and annoyed with myself. There's nothing to *be* jealous of. Cross likes me enough to put up with all of the crap I'm dragging after me, not to mention the whole complication of working as partners. It's not like he's going to dump me after ten minutes with a pretty woman in scrubs. Not that he can *dump* me, really. We haven't exactly put a label on whatever it is we are.

Should probably get around to doing that, I think. *After we figure out what the hell is happening to him.*

I hesitate outside his room and knock on the doorframe rather than walk inside. There's no reason for the pause, except that I'm unsettled and feeling awkward with the drink carrier in my hands. As he turns his attention from the TV—he's got one of the ESPN channels on—his eyes brighten and his mouth curls into an open, welcoming smile.

"What took you so long?" he asks as he shifts in the bed until he's sitting up.

I pass him the second-to-last cup of coffee in my carrier, then settle into the chair next to his bed with the final cup. "The line at the coffee shop was slower than I-90 during rush hour. I think everyone in Chicago decided to go to the same Starbucks this morning."

"Thank you for your sacrifice," he says gravely before taking a slow, steady sip, then sighing contentedly. "So, you taking me home later, or am I cleared to drive?"

"I'm pretty sure your car's still at district HQ, but if you'd rather go on your own, I can have a uniform bring it over."

He shakes his head and takes another sip. "I wouldn't mind if you took me. The doc gave me a clean bill of health last night, but I don't know... I just feel drained. Could it... Is that normal? For Mediums, I mean, after they've done their... stuff?"

"Your eloquence astounds me."

He flips me off.

Laughing, I say, "Yes, it's normal. Not that you exactly had a normal day."

"Speak for yourself, Officer Concussion."

I run my hand over my hair, as if I can still feel the injury that's been healed for days now. Even with the Healing power being a bit more temperamental than the rest of my Affinities, it's useful as hell. There's not even a lingering flinch of pain when my fingers dig into where the concrete knocked me senseless—only the smooth, uninterrupted skin of my scalp and my hair tangling around my questing fingers.

"Well," I say at last before falling into a seat next to his bed, "some of us have all the luck."

I try not to think of the penny on my kitchen floor. Cross rolls his eyes and hides behind his coffee before turning his attention back to the TV. I put up with about ten more seconds of sports before I take the remote and flip it to another channel.

He glares at me before trying to take the remote

back, but I can still see his smile as he does it. I keep the remote out of his reach, and as we play a half-hearted game of keep-away, the tension bleeds from my shoulders and his faked annoyance makes my mouth twitch up at the corners.

The commercials end, and it cuts to an anchor introducing weather and traffic on the eights. As I let his voice fade into the background, I fall into the comfortable halfway point between normal and Second-Sight. Looking at Cross, who's completely engrossed in whatever exciting traffic report is being shared on the screen, I wonder at the darkness in the center of his chest. We're three days out from when he enveloped the Turned ghost in a blanket of power, and while the psychic wound was a pinprick when they admitted him, it's grown to the size of a ragged quarter now. In Second-Sight, the margins of it are indistinct and tangled with red-black energy. As I watch, that power shifts and snaps, crackling out from the center of his chest in bright arcs of energy that taint the air with ozone and iron.

Can we Heal it? I Send to Priya as carefully controlled as I can, not wanting Cross to pick up on our conversation.

I don't know. I've never seen anything like it before. It reminds me...

I fight the urge to frown. *What?*

It reminds me of Baker. Of when the two of you fought, when you Burnt him. It... Well, it looked a bit like that.

I curse internally and drag my gaze from Cross.

That's what it looks like to me, too, though I don't like admitting it. Staring out the hospital window into the early-morning sunrise, I fight against the bile rising in my throat.

I don't regret it, I manage to say. *I don't regret saving Cross and Burning Baker. Even if I had known that this is where we'd end up, I still would've done it. It's better than Baker taking Cross over, or doing whatever he was trying to do by releasing the binding.*

No one's arguing that, Kim. But you can't pretend like everything's fine.

That's not what I'm doing.

She raises an eyebrow. *Really?*

I want to run my fingers through my hair. I want to scrub at my face and rage against her words. Instead, I sit quietly and pretend to watch TV while Cross sits, unknowing, next to me.

I just... I don't know what to do about it, okay? Baker shouldn't have been able to possess Cross in the first place, and Riley shouldn't have developed powers, much less a full-fledged Affinity. He shouldn't have been able to Burn a Turned ghost with only power. He didn't use any kind of circle, no blood, nothing. What's happening to him doesn't make sense. So, if it looks like I'm flailing here, it's because I am.

A plastic cup on Cross's bedside table falls over, spilling water onto the tabletop and the floor. Cursing, I jump from my chair and start looking for some kind of towel. There's a thin cotton blanket over his feet, so I grab that and start dabbing at the water.

"Sorry," he says, a sheepish grin covering his face. "I

must've bumped into the damned thing. I keep forgetting it's there."

"It's okay." I blot the spill ineffectually. I can't look at him. "It's just a bit of water."

I know he didn't bump into the table. His arms were by his sides, hands resting on his stomach. He was nowhere near it. Worst of all, I felt the burst of energy, the shockwave of anger, that radiated from my body and coursed through the room.

It wasn't like with the penny or the bottle cap. There was no control to it, no thought. Pure emotion whipped through me, and then the power whipped through the world. The only victim this time was a cup, but if Shaking is tied to my emotions, who's to say what will happen next? I curse myself for not thinking to bring the intro book with me. I have only a vague idea when they're going to discharge Cross, and I could've at least killed time by reading the chapter on Shakers more carefully.

Cross's attention still on the TV, I throw the blanket over the water on the floor and watch as it darkens. There's nowhere to hang it up, so I leave the blanket where it is and settle back into my chair. Slumping low in the seat, I cross my ankles before me, legs outstretched, and do my best to pay attention to the news.

I don't remember falling asleep, so waking up later is a bit of a shock. I don't know how long it's been since I dozed off, but the sun is slanting through the windows of Cross's room directly into my eyes. My phone is ringing, and Cross is saying my name insistently, like it's not the first time he's had to do it. Chasing the fog from my mind, I slap my hand against the answer button and push the phone to my ear, unsure of who's calling.

"Detective Phillips," I manage, voice rough with sleep. "How can I help you?"

"Where are you, Detective?" Lieutenant Walker's voice sets my head pounding.

"Saint Bernard." I pause. "I'm with Detective Cross."

"How's he doing?"

I raise an eyebrow at Cross, and he gives me an exaggerated thumbs-up. Rolling my eyes, I turn my attention back to the Lieutenant.

"He's fine," I say, rubbing the last of sleep from my eyes. "Healing up well. The doctors should be letting him out"—I check the wall clock, then glance at Cross with my eyebrow raised; he holds up four fingers—"in about four more hours."

"I know we didn't have a chance to debrief yesterday, what with everything that happened, but I would like you to try to explain to me what happened out there. You don't have to get technical with it, not with the ghost shit, but I need something. I mean, what the hell, Phillips?"

"There was a gas explosion—"

"I'm well aware of the explosion, Detective." She sighs down the line. "I need to know about the ghost. Since you had camera crews from most of the city's major networks there to report on the collapse, it's been all over the news. You're fucking trending on Twitter right now."

I wince. "Let me explain."

"Please do." Her voice drops. "There's also the matter of what happened with Detective Cross. We didn't get lucky enough for the news cameras to miss that, either."

I curse internally. "As for that, I can—"

"Don't try to bullshit me now, Detective. You're both on medical leave for the next two weeks."

"Lieutenant, I—"

"*You*"—her voice is knife-sharp and just as cutting—"were caught in a fucking building collapse with a serious concussion and were lucky to not be hurt worse than that. Detective Cross had some sort of… episode before passing out on live TV. You're *lucky* it's only two weeks. You should be *thanking me* that it's only two weeks. And that's not even bringing the IAB investigation into consideration. Martinez is doing what he can to clean up your mess, but you've got a pile of trouble waiting for you when you get back."

"How's that going?" I ask, body tensing at the reminder. "Cooper, I mean. I'm sure he's got a lawyer by now, but IAB has to have something on him, right?"

"Yeah, they're working him, but he's only the start. I can't promise that you won't be put on administrative leave while the brass tries to untangle that fucking mess."

I sink deeper into my chair, heart pounding. "So, you're benching me. Benching us."

"Temporarily." She sighs again. "At least until IAB gives you and Cross the all clear."

"Detective Martinez trusted us to handle things before. What's changed?"

"That's need-to-know, Detective, and you don't need to know. Not now, anyway. For the time being, I want you to focus on healing up. We'll talk about a real debrief once you get back. Don't waste the chance to get your story straight, either. I might be willing to give you the benefit of the doubt, but the higher-ups won't be, not with the way the mayor's office is breathing down their neck about this."

My mouth is dry, my throat tight. "Do you want me to tell Detective Cross, or…"

"You're with him, you can tell him. He'll probably appreciate hearing the news from you more than from me. Two weeks, Detective. I'll see you after, and I expect you to have your facts in order."

She hangs up before I can say goodbye. I let my phone rest in my hands, staring at the black screen before I gesture toward the TV.

"You're going to want to change to another channel," I tell Cross, my stomach twisting.

Walker wasn't kidding about the news coverage. The next local station has a bit of information about the explosion and building collapse on the news ticker, and they splash a graphic up about a special report airing later that night, Rivera's Turned ghost towering over emergency vehicles as the cell phone camera follows him with unsteady, shaking movements.

Twitter is rife with conjecture of what happened, and as I scroll through the still photos and short videos, I see Cross, time and time again, in the middle of the cracked parking lot, his eyes black, his body surrounded by gold, his mouth twisted in a smile I've never seen on his face. There are more than a few Mediums speaking up, too, all of them wondering what, exactly, his Affinity is and what he did to Burn the ghost. Over and over, I see that ball of power between his hands launch itself at the ghost, watch it wrap around Rivera's body and eat it away.

It reminds me of an empty graveyard and my blood smeared across a ghost's skin.

I turn off my phone and look away from the TV, away from Cross, away from the darkness seeping from his chest.

Chapter Four

C ross is discharged a few hours later with strict instructions to take it easy.

"Nothing strenuous," the doctor says after he enters another note into Cross's electronic chart. "You're not on bed rest, but you're going to be tired for the next couple of days. Don't be surprised if you end up sleeping more than usual or if you nod off in the middle of the day. It'd be best if you could have someone around"—he gives me a meaningful look—"to make sure you're taking care of yourself and to lend you a hand if you get worn down."

"I can do that," I offer, and Cross smiles at me while the doctor nods.

"Check in with your primary care doctor in two weeks if you're still feeling tired. Otherwise, you should be fine with a bit more rest."

"Thanks, Doc." Cross already has the blanket thrown back, his long legs settling on the floor with confidence. "Now, where'd they put my pants?"

The drive to Cross's apartment is nearly silent. Not because I don't know what to talk about—though I don't—but because Cross nods off after a few minutes.

His head resting against the window, mouth slightly parted in sleep, he seems fragile. My chest aches, and I make sure to take any turns slower than I normally would, glancing at him after each one to make sure he's still asleep.

When I pull up in front of his building, I have to shake him awake.

"Riley." His arm tenses beneath my hand. "Hey, we're here. Time to wake up."

He yawns. "I was just resting my eyes."

"Right, and that's why you were snoring." I get out of the car and wait for him to clamber out after me. He leans back as he stands, his lower back cracking loud enough that I can hear it over the sound of traffic. "Let's get you inside."

His apartment is as neat and tidy as ever, and I have to fight my immediate urge to start messing it up. I dutifully hang my coat on the rack by the door and leave my shoes by its base. Cross does the same, though he stumbles a bit when he kicks his shoes off.

I bend down to put his shoe in line with the others and stand. "We need to get you to bed."

"The doc said nothing strenuous," Cross says with a tired grin. "You'll have to be gentle."

I laugh. "Shut up and get your ass moving, Cross."

"Of course, Detective," he says with fake formality. "Whatever you say. I wouldn't want to contradict an officer of the law."

Glaring, I shoo him into his bedroom. As he starts

to undress, I freeze. It's not the first time I've seen Cross without his clothes on, but it suddenly feels different. His back to me, his well-muscled shoulders shifting as his shirt goes over his head, there's a vulnerability to him that makes the breath catch in my throat. I'm overwhelmed by the desire to take care of him, to put my hands on his skin not for sexual reasons, but to lift some of his burden through touch. I let the feeling wash over me, let it drag me down into a brief flash of fantasy. Of tucking him into his bed, of brushing the hair from his forehead so I can press a kiss there, of waiting for him to call me when he needs me.

Unaware of the domestic panic I'm experiencing, Cross tosses his shirt into a hamper, then turns slightly, catching me frozen in the doorway.

"You okay?" he asks, brow furrowed.

I swallow and nod. "Yeah, I'm fine. Just... I'll wait outside."

"Kim." He takes a hesitant step toward me. "Talk to me."

The scar in the center of his chest is raised and red. The center of the circle sparks and snaps with power, the black creeping into the pale expanse of his skin. Even from across the room, I can feel the sting of it along my senses. I wonder if part of my sudden desire to care for him is because I'm the cause of his injury. He wouldn't be this tired if it weren't for me. He wouldn't be in danger if it weren't for me.

I've waited too long to respond. Cross's brow starts to furrow, so I blurt out, "You just scared me. Seeing you collapse like that."

"Well," he says as he walks to stand in front of me, "you're not the only one who was scared recently." He cups my cheek, then tucks my hair behind my ear. On the tail end of the gentle touch, I feel him press against my skull. "You're all healed up, though."

"Seems like." I lean into his hand.

"I don't think…" His gaze travels across my face with a desperate mix of fear and relief. "I've never been so scared in my life, Kim. I thought…"

"Hey." I lay my hand over his. "I'm okay. We're okay."

"Just… don't do that again, okay?"

As solemnly as I can, I say, "I promise that I will never end up in a building collapse again."

It tugs a laugh out of his chest. He leans in to kiss me, slow and easy, and I fall into it as easily as I fall into Second-Sight. Warmth fills me like power. The kiss is languid and heady, simple even as it tears through me. Sighing when his lips part from mine, I smile and open my eyes, uncertain when they fell shut.

Cross's eyes are black.

My entire body tenses. He must feel it because he frowns.

"Are you sure you're okay?"

I blink, and when I open my eyes again, all I see are his green eyes filled with worry. The only black in them are his pupils, still wide from our kiss.

"I'm fine." Somehow my voice sounds normal, the

choking fear nowhere to be found. "Go on, get into bed and quit distracting me. I'll be just outside."

He rolls his eyes and darts in for another kiss. "Don't think I won't figure out what's bugging you, Phillips. I'm a trained detective and a good one at that."

"We can talk about me *after* you get some sleep. Quit stalling."

Grumbling, he climbs into his bed and settles in. The urge to kiss his forehead hits me again, but I push it down, walk out of his bedroom, and shut the door behind me.

The couch is firm and catches me easily when I fall onto it. Head cradled in my hands, I curse quietly.

You saw it? Priya asks. She's still outside of Cross's bedroom door, staring at it as if she can see through the wood. *His eyes.*

Yes.

You know what black eyes mean.

She looks at me, her own gray eyes swirling with white, then with a hint of spilled ink. The delicate skin of her cheek starts to blister and blacken, flesh consumed by fire.

Priya, I Send cautiously.

Shaking herself like a dog coming out of water, her face smooths back out, healed and whole, and when her eyes open, they're gray and unassuming. *We can't ignore it.*

No, we can't.

Priya lets me know a few minutes later that Cross is asleep. I ask her to keep an eye on him, and once I know she's settled in his room, I call Andrea.

"Hello, Detective," she says, sounding surprised. "I didn't think I'd hear from you this soon."

"What're you doing right now?"

"Nothing at the moment. Why do you ask?"

I rub at the bridge of my nose, already feeling a headache coming on. "I need you to get to Cross's apartment. There's a… complication."

"With you, when isn't there?" She sighs. "Text me his address. You're lucky I've got the day off."

"Thank you. Just a second."

I pull my phone from my face, pull up a new text message from Andrea's contact info, and quickly type in Cross's address.

"It'll take me about twenty minutes to get there. Does he know I'm coming?"

"He's asleep."

"Poor thing. Well, hopefully it won't be too much of a surprise. Do you want to try to explain what this 'complication' is before I hit the road?"

"It's…" I glance at the closed bedroom door, then tentatively reach through my bond with Priya, feeling for her attention. All I get is a general sense of distraction, as if she's not focusing on anything at all. "I think whatever is happening to Cross is affecting Priya. Earlier, I thought she might be… It doesn't make any sense. Just. Get your ass here, and let's see if we can figure something out."

Her concern is palpable as she says, "Okay. I'll see

you soon."

"Hey, Andrea," I say before she can hang up, "thank you. I didn't mean to drag you into all of this, but I don't think… Anyway, just thanks, I guess."

"You're welcome, Kim. See you soon."

"See you."

I stare at my phone until the screen goes black and place it carefully on Cross's coffee table. Settling into the couch, I fall into Second-Sight and wait.

Andrea's barely knocked on the door before I'm throwing it open. Her eyes are wide in surprise as she takes me in, a slow perusal from head to toe that makes me shift uncomfortably.

"You look like shit," she says cheerfully before pushing her way into the apartment. "Where's your partner?"

I close the door. "Still sleeping. Try to keep your voice down."

"Of course." She slips her bag from her shoulder and sets it carefully on the table. As she settles on the couch, she reaches in and starts pulling out a mountain of books. "I brought whatever I could on the fundamentals of runes and sigils. I figured we could start there since I remember it being a relatively simple mark on his chest."

"Just… Hold on a moment." Her eyebrow raises as I fumble for steady ground. "Can I get you something to drink?"

"No." She gestures to the couch. "Sit down, and tell me how Detective Cross ended up with a rune in the middle of his chest."

"I'm going to get you something to drink," I say instead, hurrying to the kitchen to grab a glass and fill it with tap water. I leave the tap running as I catch my breath, fingers tight around the glass and the edge of the sink.

"That bad, huh?"

I jump, spilling water over my fingers and into the sink.

"Christ, Andrea," I snap. "Don't sneak up on me like that."

She sighs. "Real bad. You did it, I'm guessing?"

I glare at her over my shoulder, but all it does is make her grin, quick and stinging.

"Does it matter?" I ask as I refill the glass and slam the water off. Even though the glass is supposedly for her, I take a deep drink before turning around, leaning my back against the counter.

"Considering the circumstances, probably." She takes the glass from my fingers, drinks from it, then sets it down on the counter. "So, either you can tell me about it, or I can go wake up lover boy and find out from him instead."

"You're such an ass."

"Pot, meet kettle."

Groaning, I move back to the living room. Her shoes click out an even staccato behind me. "You need to take your shoes off. He doesn't like it when people wear shoes inside."

She rolls her eyes, then kicks her heels off. They lay haphazardly on the floor next to the coffee table, and I feel the urge to pick them up and hurl them toward the door. Instead, I sit on the couch, fingers tight around my knees while Andrea settles on the other end, one knee on the cushion, her other foot on the floor. She looks easy, relaxed. Poised and elegant against Cross's too-white sofa and across from my too-tense body.

"Talk to me, Phillips," she says with steel in her voice.

Priya joins in. *She needs to know if she's going to help. She's saved your life before, Kim. You can trust her.*

The worst part is I know I can. I know that Andrea will keep this between us if I ask her to. Admitting to it, though, makes my gut twist.

"You can't tell him," I start. As she nods, hesitant but still agreeing, I go on. "Do you remember those deaths, the ones of Mediums?"

"From last year," she says, nodding. "It wasn't that long ago."

I mentally tally the months between now and then and curse to myself when I realize she's right. All it's taken is a handful of months to send my life spinning.

"There was a ghost." I swallow. "He used to be a man named Joseph Baker."

She listens intently as I do my best to explain everything that happened last November. When I get to the asylum and Cross's possession, she goes still.

"You said he was Mundane."

I nod. "He used to be."

"There's no way he could've been possessed if he was Mundane."

"Trust me," I say with a pained laugh, "I'm aware. But whatever Baker was, he didn't follow the normal rules. He took over Riley like it was nothing. I didn't even know that something was wrong at first, not until…" I swallow. "He nearly killed me. I don't know why I did it, but I put that symbol on his chest with my blood, and then…"

"And then Baker was gone, and you were still here."

"And Cross had that damned symbol burned into his skin."

Andrea sighs heavily and leans farther back into the couch, head tilted back as she thinks. "Well, it's somewhere to start. You still have that book, the one with the binding in it?"

I nod. "Not here, but I've got it at home."

"I'm going to need to borrow it. Whatever Baker was able to do before you Burnt him, it's got to be tied up in the binding. Something strong enough to cut a Medium off from their powers, something that required all the other Affinities… Well, I don't have to tell you that it's powerful."

"No, you don't."

"And what about now?" Andrea glances toward the bedroom. "What happened the other day."

"Did you see it?" I nearly choke on the words.

"I saw *something*. Not entirely sure what I saw."

"I think…" I close my eyes, take a deep breath. "Those tears that are forming all over Chicago? I think they're tied to him. Tied to his possession and that symbol. They started getting bad right after…"

Andrea shakes her head. "No, that wouldn't make sense. Those markers have been around for generations, right? If it was all down to Cross, then they wouldn't be necessary, and from what that Dave guy told us, they seem pretty fucking necessary."

I bite my lip, nodding. "It still seems suspicious to me."

"It absolutely is," Andrea agrees, "but while that Baker guy might've been a catalyst, he didn't start the whole problem." Sighing, she sits forward to shift through her books. "Well, you've definitely given me plenty to think about. Like I said, I'll see if I can find out anything about the symbol. I'll need you to draw it for me, along with any of the others you remember from that ceremony. How soon do you think I can get that book from you, by the way?"

"Tomorrow," I say as she pushes a pad of paper and pen toward me. I take both and start sketching out the symbols from the back covers. "Like I said, it's at home. I just don't want to leave Cross on his own right now."

Are you going to tell her the rest? Priya Sends. She's still in Cross's room, but she peeks her head through the door, frowning at me. *You can't expect her to do her best work without knowing all of the details.*

I've told her everything.

Have you? She raises an eyebrow. *What about your other Affinities?*

I grimace, and Andrea catches it before I can smooth out my expression.

"What?" Her tone is suspicious. "I don't like that look, Phillips."

No choice but to tell her now. Priya's smiling when she ducks through the door, and I Send a lance of annoyance through our bond. Her laugher is high and delighted, and I barely stop myself from sticking my tongue out at her.

"There's… Christ, there's more that you need to know."

She raises her brows. "There's more than a Turned Medium, an underground secret society, and a generational conspiracy?"

"Yes?"

"Jesus Christ, Detective. You sure know how to have a good time."

I wince. "Look, this is hard to explain—"

"No fucking kidding."

"Could you stop interrupting me?"

She holds up both hands. "Sorry, sorry. Go on."

"I just…" Groaning, I gesture toward her bag. "Do you have anything in there that's important to you? Or that you've had for a long time?"

Frowning, she reaches into her bag and pulls out a set of keys. There's a battered keychain dangling from them, an enameled Cubs logo that has dings in the metal and a crack through the middle of the C. "My dad got it for me the first time we went to a game," she says before handing it over. "Don't fuck it up."

I sigh, then draw my blade from its ankle holster. Andrea doesn't comment as I nick my thumb and press it to the smooth surface of the keychain.

The Reading wants to drag me under, but I fight it, keeping myself half in, half out of it. I can smell hot concrete and popcorn, spilled beer and sweat.

"Cubs were down by three runs," I murmur. "Bottom of the ninth, bases loaded, two outs. I can't make out the uniform—you were clearly not paying attention—but the guy at bat knocked it into right field, just shy of a foul. Winning run. Your dad was so excited, he spilled his beer on the guy in the row in front of you, but he didn't care. They ended up hugging, both of them covered in Bud Light. He smelled like it the whole bus ride home. Your mom was furious."

"Holy fuck," she whispers, her eyes wide. "You can Read."

"And Heal and Speak," I say as I watch the last of my blood burn away from her keychain. I pass it back and pretend to not notice that her fingers are shaking when she takes it from me. "And Shake."

"Jesus."

"Yeah."

"For how long?"

"Since Baker."

"Well, shit." She pushes her keys into her bag and leans back. "That's fucked up."

"Yeah, you're telling me."

"So, what? You think you're going to get all of them?"

I shrug, feeling sick. "Maybe. Priya seems to think so."

"Well, that's definitely not normal." Looking at her books for a long time, she curses. "I'm going to have to go to the Newberry for that. I haven't read anything *ever* about Mediums with more than one Affinity."

I bite my lip, uncertain. "Actually," I say slowly, "I know of one."

"You can't count yourself, Phillips."

"Not me. Dave."

"Dave." Her face is blank. "The ghost at Oak Woods."

"Yes."

"And why are we trusting some random dead guy to be telling the truth?"

"Why would he lie? When he mentioned it, he thought that Priya and I were part of his little secret group. He wanted to commiserate. It wasn't until he figured out that we didn't know what he was talking about that he clammed up."

"Well, if you've got a source on this shit, why are you coming to me with it?"

"He won't talk to me. Can't get a word out of him."

She smiles. "It's that charm of yours, Kim. Always

blowing them away."

I glare while Priya laughs from the other room. Glancing her way, I lean forward, gesturing for Andrea to come closer.

"There's something going on with Priya, too," I whisper. "I noticed it at the building site, but it was worse this morning. It's almost… It's like she's Turning."

Andrea frowns. "That can't happen. You're bonded."

"I know. But her eyes were black, and her skin… She died in a fire, and it looked like she had burns."

"That's…" Andrea looks over her shoulder, then back to me. "You think it's connected to what's happening with you?"

"Or the tears or Riley. We're surrounded by that red shit. I can't be the only one who's affected by it."

"No, probably not." Andrea looks at her books again and sighs. "Definitely time for a trip to the Newberry. What're you going to do?"

"Well," I say, "I'm on leave for the next two weeks, so I figured I'd try to wear Dave down, get him to tell me anything useful. He's the best lead I've got."

"Okay. I'll see what I can find at the research library while you work on your people skills. What do you want to do about Detective Cross?"

"Any chance you know how to close one of those tears? You ripped one open before."

She gives me a rueful smile. "It's a pretty big

difference between breaking something and putting it back together."

"Well, if you think of something. Whatever's happening to him, it's hurting him, and I... Let me know if you think of anything."

"Yeah, of course. I like him, too, you know." She pushes her books around and hands one to me. "That's got a bit on the foundations of runes and sigils, the reasons why they work the way they do. Might help you get a handle on what's going on with the rune."

"Thanks." I hold the book in my lap. "And for coming over on short notice."

"Look, I know you didn't like me at the beginning, but I don't hate you or anything. You're growing on me." She grins. "Like mold."

Laughing, I flip her off. "Oh, fuck you."

"If only you were so lucky." After collecting the rest of her books and packing them back up, she stands. "I'll call you once I find out more. Give my best to the detective."

"Will do."

I see her out, closing the door behind her and locking it. When I peek into Cross's room, he's still passed out, his back to me and his breathing even and steady. Leaving the door cracked so it's easier for me to hear him if he calls, I lean back and get comfortable on the couch, Andrea's book perched on my knees. I try reading it for a few minutes, but each page is drier than the last and by the time I get through the first section of the introduction, my eyes are heavy. I drift off somewhere in the middle of a semantic argument the author is having with themselves and count my blessings.

Chapter Five

The ringing of my phone wakes me early the next morning. Fumbling for it, I blearily read the screen, then roll out of bed. Cross reaches for me as I do, but I dodge his hand and step into the hallway to answer the call.

"Taka. What do you want?"

I can sense his irritation coming through the phone line. "I know you're mad at me, Kim, but that is no reason to be rude."

"How can I help you, sir?" I grit out. It's too early for this shit.

Taka's voice is as sharp as mine. "I wouldn't have called you, except that it's an emergency. There's an *onryou* in Gary, right past the Indiana-Illinois border, in an abandoned industrial park. I would go myself, but I am still trying to find out more about Ruth's organization and their plans in the city. I was hoping you might have time to Burn it, before it becomes a danger to the public."

"How bad is it?" I ask. I might still be furious with him, but my feelings take a back seat to a Turned ghost on the loose.

"It attacked a security guard last night. There weren't any serious injuries, but that was due to luck rather than the ghost's desire to not cause harm."

"You figure, what? Another two days at the most?"

He pauses, thinking. "Maybe less. Ghosts have been Turning much faster as of late. I don't think we can base its timeline against what we might consider normal."

I walk into the kitchen to check the time. It's early, much earlier than I expected. I don't have anything happening today, other than more research and possibly going to Oak Woods. A Burning will get me out of the house, get me some space from Cross, bring some sense of normalcy back into my life.

"Okay," I say, "but I'm not doing it for you. I'm doing it to help the ghost and the people it might hurt. This isn't me forgiving you."

"Of course not." He sounds angry and sad. "I am still trying to find out more about what Ruth is trying to accomplish in the city. I will call you when I know more."

"Good. Text me the address. I'll head that way in a half hour."

"Thank you, Kim, and good luck."

I hang up the phone without saying goodbye.

I dress quickly, while Cross remains curled up in the bed. He's pressed his face into the pillow, with one eye peering out and watching me as I move around the room.

"Are you going into district HQ?" he asks, his voice muffled by the pillow.

Bent over and halfway through putting on a sock, I nearly fall over at his question. I finish stuffing my foot in, then stand, still feeling unsteady.

"Actually, about that…"

"I figured, I'm on medical leave," he says. His eye falls shut. "I haven't been able to do much more than sleep since I was admitted to the hospital. But you're doing fine, and I know there's got to be a fuckton of paperwork to get through."

"I'm on leave, too," I interrupt. "Walker called yesterday. I meant to tell you then, but it slipped my mind with getting you discharged and settled."

He's quiet for a long moment, and I brace myself for his anger. Instead, his shoulders fall as he exhales, the sound muffled by the pillow. "I figured as much from your call with her yesterday. I couldn't make out much of it, but between what you were saying and what was on the news, I didn't think she'd be welcoming us back with open arms."

"We haven't been fired."

"Close enough." He grunts as he turns onto his side, looking at me full on. "This isn't the same kind of coverage as we got with Jackie Harris. I bet the brass is furious."

"Plus there's Cooper and what he was getting up to." I twist my mouth into a wry smile. "At least you'll have plenty of time to rest."

"So, where are you going?"

I sigh. "There's a ghost in Gary that needs Burning."

"And there's no one else close enough to handle it?"

"Not really." I grab my phone from where I set it on the bedside table and tuck it into my pocket. "It's nothing I haven't dealt with before. I'll be back before you know it."

"Try not to do anything dangerous, okay?" He sits up, the blanket falling away to reveal his chest. Distracted only a moment by firm muscle and smooth skin, my eyes are drawn to the mark. The wound is slightly larger today, his skin stained an angry red. "I won't be there to drag your ass out of trouble."

That's why I'm here, Priya offers, trying to break the sudden tension in the room. *I'll keep an eye on her, Riley.*

"Someone has to." As I turn to go, he calls out to me. "Hey, come here."

I roll my eyes, then dutifully walk over to the bed. His hand is warm and firm on the back of my neck as he pulls me in for a slow, drugging kiss. I lose myself to it, eased by the familiar thrill of his mouth against mine. I taste his smile before pulling away. His eyes glitter, green and bright.

"Go back to sleep." I push him back down, and he goes with it, laughing as he bounces slightly on the mattress. "I'll be back before you know it."

"Have fun in Gary!"

I roll my eyes again. "Said no one ever. I'll call you

when we're on our way back."

He hums quietly, then pulls the blankets back over his shoulders. I indulge myself for a moment, looking at his bed-mussed hair and sleepy eyes, then head out, softly closing the bedroom door behind me.

Though it's a bit out of my way, I swing by my apartment after leaving Cross's place. I'll grab the book for Andrea and a change of clothes. After throwing a handful of clean clothes into a duffel bag where I keep some extra Medium supplies, I get back in the car and on the road.

The drive to Gary is dull and tedious. The roads are clogged with commuters, and I find myself stuck in stop-and-go traffic more than once. As odd as it is, I'm comforted by the familiar irritation of slow-moving cars and the raucous chorus of horns splitting the early-morning air.

At least some things are predictable.

The industrial park is gated and locked when we arrive. There's a small shelter with a plexiglass window and a tired-looking man in a rumpled security company uniform sitting inside. I grab my Medium credentials from my glove box, then get out of the car and walk over.

"Morning," I say, drawing his attention away from a miniature TV nestled in the corner of his desk. "I hear you've got a ghost problem."

He squints at my credentials and lets out a relieved sigh. "Glad you're here, ma'am. He's been nothing but trouble for the last two weeks. Scaring the night crew, knocking shit over, all of that stuff, but he didn't get violent until last night. Nearly took Kenny's head right off. You should've seen the gash." He shakes his head. "Best get him moving on, is what I say. Let me get the gate for you, just a minute."

He takes a set of keys from the wall, exits the booth, and walks to the gate. The lock falls open easily, and he pushes the gate open for me, oddly gallant as he bows slightly with his back to the gate.

"You won't be able to miss him. Keep heading straight back and turn left at the building with the big C on it. It's the only empty building in the place, so it's not hard to miss."

"Thanks"—I look at his nametag, then back to his face—"Adam. Have a good morning."

"You, too!"

The gate closes behind me, the chain rattling as Adam locks it with easy, practiced motions. I try not to think about my main exit being blocked off and continue forward. It's still dim out, the sun hiding beneath the horizon and behind the empty buildings of the industrial park. There's no one else in the park with us, and Priya and I move through the pensive silence cautiously, listening for the ghost.

It doesn't take us long to find him. He sits on the top of a building, his legs dangling over the edge as he stares down at us. His eyes are shadowed by his brow, their color uncertain in the gloom. His neck, though, is twisted awkwardly and bruised in a thick line that disappears under the hook of his jaw.

Looks like he hung himself, I Send to Priya. *You want to try talking to him?*

Before she can respond, he slides from the edge of the building, dropping with painful speed before jerking to a stop against the side of the building, his body swaying as if held up by a rope. It bumps against the large letter C, spinning from the contact. The ghost twists in slow circles, but I can sense his eyes on me even as he moves.

I don't like the feel of this, Priya Sends. Her hair is rising around her face, and her eyes are fractured with white energy as she gathers it into herself.

Me neither. The stick of chalk in my pocket is a small comfort. I roll it between my fingers before pulling it out. *You think we'll have time to get a circle down?*

Maybe.

The ghost slows its pendulous swing, its incorporeal body resting heavily against the concrete wall. A moment later, it disappears. Footsteps echo between the buildings, and as I draw my eyes upward, I see the ghost pacing along the roofline again.

I start scribing.

Chalk scrapes along the tarmac. With the familiar friction buzzing in my hand, I sketch out a Burning circle I've used a hundred times before. It flows from me with long, practiced strokes, each symbol falling into place with ease. Whatever might be happening with me and with Cross, at least this is easy.

He's moving again, Priya Sends as I finish the final symbol. Glancing over my shoulder, I watch the ghost drop from the side of the building again, see the painful lurch and the sickening swing.

Why does he keep doing it? I ask before standing. *You'd think he wouldn't want to relive it, that he'd stop.*

I don't know. We haven't had to Burn many suicides.

She's right. Most of the time, suicides pass on as soon as they die. They've gotten what they wanted, after all. But as I watch the ghost's body swing, I wonder.

I glance at Priya, then Send to the ghost. *What are you doing?*

Eyes flashing, he tries to drop his lifted chin to look directly at me. *What does it fucking look like I'm doing?*

Killing yourself, I Send, wishing I'd palmed my knife before starting this conversation. Priya glares at me. *But why do you keep doing it?*

Through gritted teeth, the ghost says, *Because it didn't work.*

Of course.

You know you're dead, right?

He starts laughing, though his mouth doesn't move. As his swing comes to a stop, his back presses against the wall and his eyes lock on me.

If I'm dead, how am I talking to you? Why can I feel how cold it is? Why am I hungry?

Unease snakes its way through my veins. He shouldn't be able to feel *anything.*

You want it all to end? I take a step closer, my neck aching as I look up at the ghost. *If you come down here instead of going back up, I can make that happen.*

He stares at me as best he can, and when he disappears this time, he reappears at the base of the wall instead of atop it. The ghost's head hangs limp and unsteady against his shoulder, the broken spine pressing against the skin. As he draws closer, his steps are uneven and stumbling, and his hands flex spasmodically by his sides.

Up close, it's clearer that this was a kid. He's got a thin dusting of hair along his upper lip, and some of the unsteadiness of his movements is due to the coltish length of his arms and legs.

So, the ghost says with all the snark of a teen, *what're you going to do?*

I walk toward the circle and gesture for him to follow me. Clearly apprehensive about it, he trails after me, his gray eyes darting from me to the chalk on the ground.

Stand here. I'll put a bit of power into this circle, and then you'll cross over.

Cross over?

Into Death. My eyes still locked on him, I kneel down to ease my knife from my boot. *The Other Side. Whatever you want to call it.*

Will it hurt?

I hate that question.

I prick my thumb before answering. *I don't know, kid.*

My blood smears into the chalk, a stark slash of red against the white and black. Light erupts from the circle, a twisting mass of blue-white-red-green-yellow-orange.

The ghost takes a step back.

I don't... Are you sure?

Been doing this for a long time. You can trust me.

His eyes suddenly swirl with black. Blood trickles from the corners of the ghost's mouth, and he takes another stumbling step back. *I can't trust anyone. No one listens.*

Shit.

Priya, you ready?

She appears by my side, body crackling with energy. *And waiting.*

No one can help me. The voice is different, wet and raspy, the ghost's death manifesting in his words. His eyes swirl darker until they're fully black. *They all lie.*

Shit, shit, shit.

I pull power and hurl a sheet of it toward the ghost. He lurches to the side, and the wave of energy splashes into the building behind him.

Rope appears around the ghost's neck and tangles its way down his arms until it trails on the ground. The loose end twists and curls its way toward Priya before striking at her feet like a coiled serpent. Dodging to the side, she throws her own blazing power at the ghost. The rope lashes out at it, whip-fast, and the binding disappears in a flash of white.

Rocks and debris rise around him, swirling in small eddies. I throw up a shield, then flinch as bits of gravel start pinging against it in bright sparks.

I warned them, the ghost continues. The bruise around

his neck darkens into a deep purple around the edges with a band of white in the center where the rope bit in the hardest. As he rolls his eyes, his head slips to the side. Something inside cracks like a gunshot, and I flinch. *I told them what would happen.*

A larger piece of rubble comes winging toward me, and I fling my hand out in front of me on instinct, even though I know the shield should catch it. Instead, orange light crackles from my hand, and the baseball-sized piece of concrete stops in midair. I can feel it in my grasp, even though it's nowhere within reach. Staring, I rotate my wrist and watch as the stone twists with the motion.

I grin and chuck the rock back at the ghost. It whips through the ghost's form harmlessly but startles the ghost enough that the other rocks and bits of concrete around him tumble to the ground with a sound like rainfall.

Tentatively, I reach out with that same orange power and sweep away the debris in a huge push. It scatters in a circular wave, skittering and jumping across the tarmac. The ghost's eyes follow the wave of stones, then dart back to me. Around his arm, the rope tightens.

The coiled length lashes out. I push it away with a wave of orange energy, then follow it with a blast of blue-white. The binding grabs onto the rope, then flows up the twisted strands until it wraps around the ghost's arm. Screaming, the ghost tries to throw the power off, but the blue-white light keeps moving, covering the ghost's shoulder first, then wrapping around his chest until his whole body is enveloped in light.

Please, he moans, *I just want it to be over. Please, let it be over.*

I reach with orange again and pull the ghost closer. Though his feet skid and skip over the tarmac, I manage to drag him right outside the glowing circle.

That's what I'm here to do, I Send, trying to calm the ghost down. He only struggles harder. Cracks start to form in the binding. *Look, if you step into the circle, it'll be done with. You'll be done with Life. I promise.*

His black eyes rise to meet mine, and though I want to flinch away from his gaze, I refuse to give in to the desire. Blood trickles from the corner of the ghost's mouth, and his bent neck swings in sickening arcs before settling against his chest.

Let me help you.

Tendrils of orange wrap around his feet, and with my hand curled into a tight fist, I pull the ghost into the circle.

His hair lifts in a blaze of light, his head tilting back, mouth open, eyes closed. I watch as his neck settles back into place, the bruises fading. After a moment, the ghost turns to me with gray eyes. He seems too young for this, and with nausea rising, I'm reminded of Emma Murphy and an empty warehouse.

I blink, and when I open my eyes, the light and the ghost are gone.

That wasn't so bad, I shakily Send to Priya, who's hovering at the side of the building, her hair still

whipping around her head and her eyes still crackling
with power.

You're going to want to see this, Kim.

Frowning, I walk over to where she's peering into
the building's interior. There's no door nearby. I
clamber up a bit of concrete that's fallen from the
structure and peer into a window that's missing its glass.
It's too dark to see inside, but when I drop into Second-
Sight, the world erupts in color.

Red and black.

Oh fuck.

Staring at it, I'm shocked I don't feel the dark
energy's painful touch. *The concrete must be insulating it*, I
say. When I pull myself up into the window and lean
slightly inside, it's like an electric current through my
hands and arms. I fall back with a curse, then stumble
before catching my balance. *Fuck, how's there so much of it?*

I don't know. It's… Can you feel it?

Yeah. I rub at my still-stinging hands. *Yeah, I can feel
it.*

Priya drifts closer to the window. Her hands are
resting at her sides, and as I watch, her fingers start to
blister.

Priya… You feeling okay?

She looks down at me, and her eyes look like an oil
spill. Black swirls with gray, and I force myself to keep
my ground when all I want to do is fall back.

Shit. Shit shit *shit*.

We should go. I hold my hand out for her, and she

stares at the offer. There's something alien to the tilt of her head, the placid expression across her face, her too-still body. *Priya, we need to go.*

She turns away from me and floats closer to the building.

Fuck.

I don't know how to get rid of the power without a marker nearby. I don't know how to get Priya to come with me without attacking her, and the thought of that makes me sick. I could try leaving, stretch the bond between us until Priya's either forced to come with me or it breaks, but there's a part of me that isn't certain she won't let it fracture between us if I try too hard. Something about the energy is drawing her in, and even though I know she loves me, something in her loves that power, too.

Like a bolt of lightning through the top of my head, I get a brilliantly stupid idea. There's no guarantee it'll work. Nothing in our combined experience would say that it would. But I think about the energy that trickled through the remains of an office building and the way it faded.

Priya, I say, trying to warn her without warning her. *Let's go.*

It makes her turn and drift toward me a few precious feet. She's close to the building, but far enough that the rubble shouldn't bother her.

Probably.

With a deep breath, I start pulling power. Orange light fills my fists, then seeps up my arms and into my shoulders and chest. It fills my lungs with snapping force and shakes my bones like a low rumbling machine. Sinking into my belly and my hips, tripping through my legs and into my feet, the power fills me until it's overflowing. My teeth are chattering, and the whole world vibrates around me.

What are you doing? She tilts her head, black-gray eyes swirling.

I lift my shaking arms, tilt my palms up, and grab the air. The building before me groans.

Saving you.

I *pull* with every bit of power in my body. My back twinges, then aches. Muscles scream and wrench. Agony lances through me, but even as tears fill my eyes, I don't let go. Again, the building groans and cracks, and something snaps in my lower back. Groaning, I pull and pull.

There's a rumble in the ground, and a moment later, the wall closest to us collapses in on itself, the roof tumbling forward in a twisting slide. I curse and stumble back, my grip on the building and the power slipping. Concrete crashes to the ground next to me, and I throw my hand up, shielding against the incoming collapse. My heart is racing, mind whirling with the too-recent memories of crushed confinement and, nauseous, I throw power toward the building and try to hold it.

Everything stills, then stops. Tons of concrete and twisted rebar hover in the air, the mass of it groaning quietly as I fight against gravity. Sweat trickles down my face.

What… Kim, what're you doing?

There's a rush of cool, clear power flowing through my body as Priya pushes her gathered energy through our bond and into me.

Give me a second, I Send. My legs and back ache as I shift back. I take careful steps out of the shadow of the rubble, not stopping until I feel the comforting heat of the early-morning sun on my skin. With a sigh, I let it all go.

Probably not the smartest thing I've ever done. Dust billows from the collapse, flowing over me in a gritty cloud. I shield my eyes and peer over the limited protection of my arm to stare at the remains of the empty warehouse.

Priya wheels in front of me, her eyes wide and comfortingly gray. *What were you thinking?*

I don't… I fall into Second-Sight and breathe out in relief. The red-black power is already dissipating, broken up by cracked concrete and crumpled metal. *It had to be done.*

You had *to demolish a building?*

Yes.

She groans. *Kim, what the actual fuck?*

Do you not remember? I look at her unblemished hands. *At all?*

I remember you Burnt the ghost and we were getting ready to leave.

And the power?

Her brow furrows. *What power?*

I need to figure this shit out. Shaking my head at the thought, I start walking toward the gate. *We'll talk about it later. I think it's time we went to see Dave.*

What? Priya flies in front of me, and I walk through her, shivering at the cold touch. *Don't you dare ignore me.*

Maybe it's the close call, maybe it's the tone of her voice when she says it, but fear trickles down my spine in a cold wash at her words. When I glance at her from the corner of my eye, though, her angry glare is unstained, her arms unburned.

I keep walking.

Adam is not nearly as happy to see me when he opens the gate.

"The hell happened?" He peers over my shoulder at the cloud of dust visible through the other buildings. "That was a hell of a crash."

"You're going to want to call your insurance company," I answer, stepping past him and hurrying to the car. "But you won't have any more ghost problems."

"Insurance?" Panic crosses his face. "Wait, what're you—"

His words are cut off as I slam my car door shut. Turning on the engine, I start backing out of the parking lot. He chases after me for a moment before running a hand through his thinning hair and looking back over his shoulder toward the gate.

I feel a bit guilty, but there's no way I could've left that growing collection of energy unprotected or uncontained. It might not have been the best way to go about solving the problem, but it's done now. That should be the end of it, at least here.

Hopefully, there'll be answers waiting for us at Oak Woods.

CHAPTER SIX

T he silence in the car is oppressive. Priya stares at me from the passenger seat, her arms crossed and her mouth turned down into a frown. I do my best to ignore her, but I can feel her eyes like a persistent itch on my skin. Eventually, I break.

Look, I Send, hands tight on the steering wheel, *I had to do it.*

You're going to be lucky if they don't bring you up on charges for reckless endangerment and destruction of property.

If they do, they do. I had my reasons for it.

Ones you're not going to share with me.

I glance at her, then back to the road. My shoulders creep closer to my ears; my muscles tense. *It's complicated.*

I don't like it when you keep secrets from me, Kim.

For what it's worth, I don't like keeping them, either.

She sighs, and as her gaze turns from me to the road, her frown turns sad. *I just... I want to keep you safe, and I don't know how to do that when you don't talk to me.*

Guilt is a sharp dagger in my gut. *Can you trust me? Just for a little while longer?*

You'll tell me, though? Eventually?

Of course, I Send. I hope I'm not lying.

Then I guess I can wait. She tilts her head down and looks at me from under her brow. *But I'm not promising that I won't be impatient.*

I huff out a laugh. *Hopefully we'll both have answers soon.*

About that… Why do you think that Dave's going to start talking?

I check my mirror and merge onto an off-ramp. *We've got a few new weapons in our arsenal now. For one, we've got Taka's information, for what it's worth, and I've gained a few more Affinities since we last saw him. If I had to guess, that alone would get him to talk.* I laugh without much amusement. *Being a freak should pay off.*

You're not a freak.

I'm a bit of a freak.

Priya sighs. *Only a little bit.*

If it gets us the information we need, I can live with it.

I pull through the great green gates of Oak Woods and drive toward Dave's final resting place. It's still early enough that there aren't many people around, but as we go deeper into the cemetery, I see a few families clustered around graves, flowers in hand and bodies bowed with the weight of grief.

I pull off to the side, park, and trudge toward the base of the obelisk. The pool of power is still massive, and it pricks and stings against my body as I draw closer. Dave is perched at the top of the monument again, and as I come to the edge of the pool, he waves at me jauntily.

Hey, kid, he says as he pushes himself from the top of the obelisk to fall slowly to the ground. *To what do I owe the pleasure?*

Same shit, different day, I say with a smile. Even though he's an obstinate bastard, I can't help but like the guy. *I'm hoping you're in the mood for a chat this lovely morning.*

He scans the surrounding graves and their distinct lack of people or ghosts, then looks back to me. *Considering you're my only opportunity for conversation, your chances are certainly better than they have been.*

No tourists to scare?

None lately, he says with more than a bit of unhappiness in his voice. *It's been pretty damned dull.*

Well, let me help you out, then. I hold my arms out, welcoming. *I'm all ears.*

He scoffs. *Like you don't want something in return.*

Just a few answers to a few questions. Nothing serious.

Only if you don't have more questions about the whole—he gestures vaguely—*situation.*

Irritation builds in my chest. *Then I guess we're done talking.*

Hey, don't get pissy with me. I told you before, I can't talk about it.

And I don't have anyone else to talk to. I don't need you to tell me everything, just what you know about Mediums with multiple Affinities. Hell, I'd be happy if you told me about yourself, as long as you explain a little of how and why.

He sighs before sitting. Arms draped over his knees, he looks forlorn and tired. *I like you, Detective, really. You seem like a… Well, I don't want to say a sweet kid, 'cause you don't seem like a sweet anything, but you're smart. That's part of the problem. I have a feeling if I tell you anything, you're going to start putting it together.*

I promise, I'm not nearly as smart as you think I am.

He laughs. *Don't sell yourself short.*

I drop down and lean my back against a nearby headstone, mirroring Dave's pose. For a long moment, we stare at each other from across the boundary of the pool of red-black energy, neither of us speaking or moving.

What if I told you I had more than two Affinities?

He laughs. *Then I'd call you a liar.*

Giving him a considering look, I reach for my knife. *Promise you won't fight me?*

Depends on what you're planning to do, kid.

I'm going to show you a few things, that's all. I hold my hands, palms up, my knife resting gently in my right hand. *No funny stuff, promise.*

Eyes squinted in distrust, he leans forward. *You promise?*

Scout's honor.

Okay, he says with trepidation lingering in his tone. *Go ahead.*

I ever tell you my Affinity? I ask as I start drawing power into my body. The surface of the pooled energy ripples as if stirred by a wind, but the small waves hit the boundary and fall back. Dave's eyes watch the movement carefully, then go back to me.

No.

Burner, I say before forming a ball of blue-white energy between my hands. *Been doing it since I was a kid. Don't struggle, and this won't hurt.*

He freezes as I throw the energy at him, his mind processing what's about to happen but his body not responding fast enough. The binding wraps around him in a sheet of light and coalesces around his wrists in two bright manacles.

Neatly done, he says as he twists his arms around. *Guess you're going to force it out of me, then?*

I shake my head and let the binding fall away.

He shakes his hands out, wincing. *Felt a bit like pins and needles. Kind of wish I didn't know that.*

I never imagined it felt good. I hold my knife up, twisting it to catch the light. *Like this won't.*

I press the blade to the center of my palm and hiss as I draw it across. Ruby red blood pools in my hand, slowly trickling over the side to fall onto the ground. I hold my bleeding hand up so he can see it and reach for the tangled green energy waiting in my gut.

Vine-like tendrils of power wind their way up my arm and around my hand, digging their tips into the cut. Wincing, I hold tight control over the power as it slowly stitches the torn skin back together. When it's done, there's not even a scar to show where the cut was.

That's two, Dave says quietly. *What else are you going to do?*

Reading isn't an option, and Speaking is… Well, I'm

already doing it, so there's nothing to demonstrate. Eyeing the monument, I consider toppling it, if only for the drama of it. But I've performed one wanton act of destruction today. There's no need for a second.

Instead, I shift my focus to the pile of cannonballs sitting nearby. Orange flickers in my hands, and I reach out and grab the top-most cannonball from the pile. It doesn't budge. Gritting my teeth, I pull, and something snaps. A moment later, the cannonball rises into the air before I bring it over to Dave and set it down next to him.

That was welded on, he says quietly, his gray eyes studying me.

That's three Affinities I can show you. I can also Read and Speak.

His voice shakes. *Right. Of course.*

You want to talk now?

I'm not sure. He places his hand on top of the cannonball and sighs when it passes straight through to the ground. *This is probably a bad idea.*

The fun ones always are.

He smiles like he doesn't mean to before his expression settles into something more contemplative. *Five. Christ.*

All within the last six months.

His head jerks up, and his eyes are wide with fear. *What?*

It started last November and hasn't stopped since. For all I know, I'm going to get all of them.

That's... I watch his throat bob as he swallows. *Fuck, that's bad.*

I wouldn't know.

Climbing to his feet, he hurries to the base of the monument and scans it with terrified eyes. I watch his mouth move as he talks quietly to himself and paces around the obelisk. He stops on the side farthest from me, but I don't shift to keep him in view.

I have a feeling he's coming back.

A few tense minutes later, he hurries over to the edge of the pool, as close to me as he can get without crossing the boundary.

What do you know about Life and Death? he asks me. *And not in a theoretical sense. What do you* know *about it?*

I frown. *I mean... Life is this*—I gesture around me—*and Death... isn't?*

He shakes his head with a sigh. *Training really has gone to shit, hasn't it? I don't mean life*—he gestures around us mockingly—*I mean capital-L Life. The energy that keeps you here, that ties you to the physical world and the things within it.*

I... I don't...

Okay, great. Square one, then. He bites his lip, clearly thinking hard. *Every living thing has a power to it. Doesn't matter if it's a plant or a person, we've all got something that keeps us moving forward. Some people call it a soul, others view it as a biological process. Whatever it is, it's what makes your heart beat and your lungs breathe and your brain work. That is Life.*

And Death's the absence of that energy?

He sounds embarrassed for me when he says, *No.*

You know what Death is, even if you don't know-it-*know-it. It's what makes you a Medium. It's what keeps me and your partner in this world. It's another force, another energy, but it's not the same as Life. Think of them like siblings. They're similar. They come from the same place, but they're not the same.*

And they're antithetical to each other.

More or less. They can work in concert, but they're corrosive to each other. Life eats at Death, and Death eats at Life. It's why ghosts Turn, and it's why too much of Death lingering in Life creates anomalies.

So what does that have to do with having Affinities?

Mediums have the special ability to channel both energies at once. They contain both Life and Death within themselves, and rather than the two destroying each other, they work together. The way that partnership manifests is your Affinity.

I frown, confused. *How could you end up with more than one, though? It sounds like it should be impossible.*

While there are some genetic components, it's also dependent on how much contact with Death the Medium has. The more contact...

The more Affinities?

He nods. *Exactly. But it takes a lot of contact with Death to trigger a second Affinity in a Medium. The energy wants to go through the channel it's already established in the Medium, the existing Affinity. Splitting off another branch is difficult.* His expression goes cold and shuttered. *I can't imagine what it would take to trigger all of them.*

My throat tight, I swallow. *If I think of anything, I'll let you know.*

You, uh... You have any other questions?

No, I say with a shake of my head. *No, not today.*

You want to keep talking?

Again, I shake my head. He seems disappointed when I get to my feet, but he doesn't say anything else as he watches me. I wave at him half-heartedly as I leave, my mind still ringing with what he's said.

Priya hovers nearby, her expression carefully neutral. *You know what I'm going to say already, don't you?*

I do. I climb into my car and close the door, but after starting the engine, I don't do anything else. Instead, I stare at my hands on the steering wheel.

It can't be all because of Cross. The leather under my hands creaks. *He's not...*

Priya takes a long moment to answer. *Baker was.*

But Riley isn't Baker. He's not.

I'm not saying he is—

I turn to face her, fear and fury twined together like a rope around my neck. *You are. You know you are.*

Baker was in Death for a long time, and he was powerful. From what Dave said, contact with that power at the right time is all you need to become a Medium. We've never understood how Baker was able to possess Riley in the first place, and you're not the only one who's developed powers since we ran into him. We haven't been able to explain how Riley went from Mundane to Medium overnight. What Dave just told us... It makes sense.

It does. That doesn't mean I want it to.

He's not... If that's what's happening here—and I'm not saying it is—then that means Cross is leaking power from Death.

You've seen his chest, Kim. What else could it be?

We're not talking about this.

And ignoring the problem is going to make it go away? Priya sighs. *I know it's not exactly what you want to hear, Kim, but if we're right, then you know what we have to do.*

No, I snap, *I don't.*

Kim... Her voice is so gentle, it hurts.

You mean cut off his connection to Death. My stomach twists. *Bind him? Like they Bound Baker?*

Maybe, maybe not.

I can't... You saw what it did to Baker, how it twisted him. And you want to do that to Riley?

I don't want to do anything we don't have to. But whatever is happening to him, it's impacting the both of you, and it's not all sunshine and roses. You saw what happened to him at the crime scene when he went after that ghost? That can't be a coincidence.

We still don't know what happened there.

Then we owe it to Riley to find out.

I pull the seat belt across my shoulder angrily, clicking it shut with too much force. *Let's go talk to Andrea. I need to take her the book anyway.*

You think she'll have something already?

It's better than what we're considering, I say with a quick glance in her direction.

She makes a quiet sound of agreement, but her expression seems less confident.

As I turn back onto the road, I force myself to ignore the growing unease in my gut.

CHAPTER SEVEN

N ow that morning traffic has eased up, the drive to Andrea's place isn't nearly as bad as the drive this morning. I make good time on the highways, and even the side streets aren't too crowded. It only takes a half hour to get there, which is somewhat of a godsend considering how far I had to go. It's a bit of a relief, not having to fight my way through bumper-to-bumper traffic.

Even though my mood's marginally better, I don't feel any less uneasy about what Dave told us than when we left Oak Woods. Still, I tamp the fear down as best I can before I get out of the car and hurry to the door. I ring Andrea's apartment, and she buzzes me in without saying a word.

"Very safe," I murmur to myself as I pull the door open and head upstairs.

The building's newer and well-maintained. The elevator works, but I take the stairs anyway. She's on the third floor, which isn't that much of a walk, and I need to do something to burn off my anxiety.

Andrea's door is propped open, and though I knock before pushing it open, I can't help but sigh at her lax security measures.

"You can't leave your door open like that, Andrea," I say, shutting the door behind me. "You're going to get robbed."

"No one's going to rob me." Wearing a workout shirt and a pair of baggy harem pants, she walks into the front room, her bare feet padding softly across the wood floor. "I knew you were coming, so I left the door open. It's not something I do every day."

"Better not be," I say offhandedly, too distracted by her place now that I'm looking at it.

The few times I considered what kind of place Andrea would live in, I assumed it would be something that looked like a highly polished Instagram post: white granite countertops, gold accents, too many tiny pots with bright green succulents. Instead, there are oriental rugs spread across the floor, with an overstuffed, dark brown couch and decorative pillows covered in geometric designs. The whole place is light and airy, all of the patterns somehow playing nice with each other, and the open floor layout means that I can see into the relatively modern and sedate kitchen. There are plants tucked into the corners and on bookshelves, but they're large, draping ferns and broad-leafed monsteras. Not a succulent in sight. I take a step into the living room and pause.

"You have a chair shaped like a hand," I say, staring at the black molded plastic in disbelief.

She frowns. "You want to take a seat?"

I shake my head. "The couch is fine. It's just… not

what I expected."

She laughs before settling into another side chair, this one shaped like a chair rather than a hand. "Most people don't. Did you bring the book?"

"Yeah." I pull it out of my jacket and pass it to her before sitting down. "The important chapter's in the back."

She opens to the front and flips through the pages slowly. "With books like these, they're usually all important."

"The binding is in the back, though."

"And I'll get to it." She glances up, her gray eyes bright with barely concealed amusement. "Why don't you go get yourself something to drink, Detective? We're going to be here for a while."

Great.

I heave myself off the couch, the soft cushions doing their best to keep me in place, and head to the kitchen. It takes me a few tries before I find the right cabinet, and I pull out a dappled glass cup to fill with tap water. After a quick sip, I wander my way back into the front room.

Andrea's got her feet tucked up into the chair, and she's leaning over the book resting in her lap, her lip caught between her teeth. She tucks a strand of loose hair behind her ear and turns to the next page.

"Interesting stuff?" I ask.

She startles briefly, then turns her attention back to the book. "Different. Just skimming through this, it'd read like any other basic instructional book. But look"—she holds the book up so I can see where her finger is pressed against an illustration in the center of the page—"this isn't any kind of circle I've seen before, and trust me, I've seen a lot. It'll do exactly what it says it will, but it's doing it in an entirely novel way."

"Fascinating." I head back to the couch and sit. "Does it tell you anything about what might've happened to Cross?"

She sighs. "Not yet. I'm going to need a few days to read through it all and take notes."

"I don't know if we have a few days. It's getting worse."

"And I've got a job and other responsibilities that I need to take care of. Look, I want to help you, Kim, really, and I don't want anything to happen to Detective Cross. He's a nice guy. But this is going to take time to decipher, and there's nothing to be done about it."

"Okay, fine." I stare into my glass, mulling over her words. "There's got to be something we can do in the meantime, though."

She smiles at that. "Actually, I do have something I'd like to try. I started working on it last night, and I think it could help."

"What is it?"

"Hold on, let me get it."

She goes to set the book down, reconsiders it, and takes it with her as she disappears into the hallway she walked out of when I arrived. A few minutes later, she comes back, a large sketch pad in her hands.

"Take a look at this." She flips through the pages, each one covered in half-finished drawings of runes and sigils. Some look familiar, but most of them are designs and symbols I've never seen before. She stops and holds the sketchpad out to me. "I think it might be able to hold the energy back."

I stare in stunned silence at the runework spread across the page. At first glance, it looks simple, but the longer I look at the runes and how they're tied into the sigils, how the entire pattern ties together, the wider my mouth hangs.

"Andrea, this is…" I stare up at her in disbelief. "You did all of this last night?"

She shrugs like it's nothing, but her smile is smug. "I might've had some ideas after the first time you took me to see one of the markers. It's nothing."

"Nothing?" I trace my finger over the runes. "If this does what it looks like it will, it'll be a hell of a lot more than 'nothing.' I think this'll work."

"That's what I said." She's not even trying to hide the smugness now. "I may not be able to power these things myself, but I know what I'm doing."

"Clearly. Can I?" I mime, tearing the page out, and she nods.

"Go right ahead. It's for you, after all."

I carefully pull the sheet from the sketchpad, doing my best to not rip the paper too far from the bound edge. As I finish tearing it free, the corner rips. I pull the remaining piece from the glued edge, then roll the whole thing up carefully. The paper crinkles slightly in my fist as I hold it a bit too tight.

"Thanks for this." I carefully hold the rolled paper against my side as I stand. "Let me know if you learn anything from that book, yeah?"

"I'll call you as soon as I do." She bites her lip, suddenly unsteady. "You'll call me if it doesn't work? That binding?"

I swallow down the tickle of apprehension in my throat. "Yeah, but it'll work."

"Your faith is inspiring."

"Don't get used to it."

She laughs. "I wouldn't dream of it."

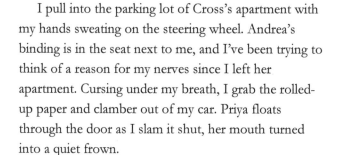

I pull into the parking lot of Cross's apartment with my hands sweating on the steering wheel. Andrea's binding is in the seat next to me, and I've been trying to think of a reason for my nerves since I left her apartment. Cursing under my breath, I grab the rolled-up paper and clamber out of my car. Priya floats through the door as I slam it shut, her mouth turned into a quiet frown.

So, what're you going to tell him?

I don't know. Something like the truth.

Her frown deepens. *Why not the whole truth? It's only going to get worse if you don't fill him in.*

Well, if this thing works, it won't get worse, and we can deal with the rest of it later.

Healthy choice, Kim. Very healthy.

I tamp down the urge to flip her off and instead head up the stairs to Cross's apartment. By the time I reach his floor, I'm out of breath and my heart is racing from more than the exercise.

I knock on the door and shift from foot to foot as I wait for him to answer it. As I prepare to knock a second time, he opens it. Cross has a gray fuzzy blanket pulled around his shoulders and neck. The color makes his cheeks look more flushed than usual, and as I unconsciously reach up to feel his forehead to test his temperature, he winces.

"Do you hear that?" he asks before sticking his head out the door and glancing down the hallway in both directions. "Someone's been screaming for the last hour, and I cannot figure out where the hell it's coming from."

Priya and I look at each other, then back to Cross.

I don't hear anything, Priya Sends.

At first, Cross doesn't say anything in response but keeps frowning at us.

"You don't hear that?" he asks. When I shake my head, he groans and steps back into his apartment. "Someone must've left their TV on too loud or something. C'mon in."

It could be ghosts, Priya offers cautiously. *But I don't feel any spirits in the building other than myself.*

I reach out with my power, probing as far as it'll

reach, but nothing pings against my senses. *Me neither.*

Priya floats after Cross as he shuffles to his couch and flops down across it, his head on the cushions, his knees pulled to his chest, his feet near the armrest. *Riley, can you hear me?*

"Only a little," he says, eyes falling shut. "You sound like a radio cutting in and out. Lots of static."

What about me? I ask, but he doesn't respond. "I'm guessing your powers have been a little off?"

"Not like they've ever behaved." He buries his chin into the blanket. "But yeah, they've gotten worse. How was Gary?"

"Great."

One of his eyes opens, the green tinged with suspicion. "That doesn't sound good."

"We Burnt the ghost and no one got hurt."

"And...?"

"And then I went to see Andrea."

"Uh-huh." He shuts his eye, but his mouth is still a flat line of displeasure. "What'd she have to say?"

"Actually"—the paper in my hand crinkles—"she might have something that'll help you."

Both eyes open, and he starts to sit up. "Really? How so?"

I wiggle the roll of paper. "This is a circle she put together. I think it'll help you start feeling better."

"So, it's something like the wards you did a couple of months ago?"

I leap at the easy explanation. "Exactly like that."

He flings the blanket off his shoulders with a flourish, smiling. "Then I'm all yours, Detective."

He's not wearing a shirt, and the mark on his chest looks like raw meat. Red and black energy nearly touches the edges of the circle, and it's smeared and streaked all across his chest. The inside of the blanket is filled with it, the power clinging to the fabric in matted clots. Now that he doesn't have the shield of the blanket, pins and needles race up my arm and into my chest. My whole body prickles and stings with it, like fire licking at kindling.

I barely hold back a wince.

Priya stares in horrified fascination.

It's worse than when we left this morning.

I know.

Kim, if his condition keeps degrading at this rate, I don—

I know.

"Let me get my chalk," I say as he wraps himself in the blanket again. He's shivering without it. "It won't be long."

My hands shake as I dig through my overnight bag. Past all of the clothes is a bottle of liquid chalk tucked into a side pocket along with a half-empty tube of toothpaste.

When I come back into the front room, Cross is sprawled across the couch, still wrapped in the blanket, his eyes closed and bruised blue underneath. I watch the subtle rise and fall of his chest for a moment, if only to remind myself that whatever is eating away at him hasn't killed him.

Not yet.

"Hey," I say, my voice unexpectedly quiet. He opens one eye and sits up.

He glares at the bottle in my hand. "It's gonna be cold, isn't it?"

"Probably."

He nods, then opens the blanket so I can see his chest. "I can put up with a bit of cold if it helps."

"It should."

As I sit on the coffee table across from him and begin tracing Andrea's binding across his skin, I hope I'm not lying.

It's more difficult to scribe than I expected. The pattern itself is intricate, but everything's complicated by the red-black energy oozing from Cross's body. It hurts when I brush my hand against it, a stinging cold that leaves my whole arm aching. It makes my marks less precise, and I have to slow down to get everything right. If Cross notices, he doesn't comment. Eyes closed, mouth open as he breathes shallowly, he doesn't say anything as I smear chalk across his skin.

By the time I finish the final mark, my arm up to my shoulder feels like it's simultaneously on fire and frozen solid. My fingers hang, limp and numb, as I pull my hand away.

Cross blinks at me, eyes half-lidded with exhaustion even though he's been resting all morning.

God, I hope this works.

"I'm going to have to power this one," I say as I reach for my knife. "It's not quite the same as the wards."

"You're going to bleed on me?"

"Wouldn't be the first time."

His laugh is more an exhalation than a sound of amusement. "Fair point."

The silver knife warms in my palm, easing some of the ache in my hand. My motions are still unsteady, though, and when I cut into the pad of my thumb, I go deeper than intended. Lemon-sharp pain sinks into my hand, and I suck in a breath as blood wells around the blade.

Quickly I bring it to the chalk on Cross's chest, then hesitate before pressing my thumb into the binding. The red oozes into the white of the chalk, and for a moment, I think it's not going to work.

Then everything explodes into too-bright light. Flinging my arm up to cover my eyes, I curse as it does nothing to block the searing brightness. The light is blue-white and green, and it digs in and clings to Cross, especially around the wound on his chest. The edges, dark and crumbling like wet, burned paper, first pinken, then knit together. My arm falls, and I stare dumbfounded as the wound heals slowly. With every inch of clean, pale flesh that creeps its way over the hole in Cross's chest, my excitement grows.

I hadn't noticed the tension Cross was carrying in his body before, but as the binding does its work, the line of his shoulders eases. He leans back into the couch, head tilted back, the long line of his neck stretched in an easy arc. His hands rest easily by his sides, and as the binding meets in the middle, sealing up the last of the hole, his entire body sags into the cushions.

"Christ." His voice is thick, his words slurred. "That's some good shit, Kim. You should bottle that."

For the first time in what feels like forever, I laugh without reservation. I stand on shaky legs and climb into Cross's lap. My hands rest on the side of his face, thumbs tracing over the curve of his cheekbones, and when he opens his eyes, the green is vibrant and warm.

"Hi," he says. His hands slide up the curve of my legs and come to rest on my thighs. "How'd you get here?"

My laugh falls into his mouth as I press our lips together. There's no pain when I press my chest against his, only the low heat of building pleasure. His hands tighten on my legs, and my blood turns molten. I shift closer in a slow, languorous roll, and he groans.

Sharp, prickling pain spears the center of my chest.

I gasp and pull away, startled by the sting.

Red-black energy trickles from the center of Cross's chest in a hair-thin trail.

"What's wrong?" Cross asks. "What happened?"

The lie tastes like copper in the back of my mouth. "Nothing. I must've pulled something at the industrial park."

"I've been told I'm quite good with my hands," he says, pressing them into my thighs. "You want me to help work it out?"

I let him lead me to the bedroom and spread me out across the bed, let him press his confident, calm hands into my muscles. Each touch aches, but it lets my mind drift enough that when he rolls me from my front onto my back, as he lowers his body over top of mine, all I feel is the pleasure of his skin against mine.

It lets me ignore the sting of the power when it drips from his body onto mine.

CHAPTER EIGHT

Later that night, curled up in bed with Cross nestled close, I can't stop myself from putting my fingers as near to the center of his chest as I can bear. The binding is still holding, but it's fighting against the red-black energy. There's a slight glow around the edges of the wound, and I trace the light with fingers that only shake a little. At my gentle touch, Cross sighs contentedly in his sleep and inches closer. I tuck my head so his mouth is nearly touching the crown of my head and let the soft breeze of his breath against my hair soothe the ache in my heart.

I follow the edges of the wound. It sparks against my fingers, tiny frissons of pain that could be forgettable if they weren't so persistent, so omnipresent whenever I put my hand anywhere near the mark. I remember the way it used to glow, bright and warm, and the peace I found when I touched it. The sense of belonging, of place.

That sensation isn't gone. Cross hasn't done anything to make me feel less welcome in his arms, in his bed. He hasn't complained, though I know he's tired and confused. He hasn't pushed me away, even when he should have. It's nothing more than what I deserve, but he insists on giving me everything I don't. He smiles at me and presses gentle kisses to my skin, my mouth, holding me with steady hands. He makes me feel weak, and he makes me enjoy that weakness.

I drop my head to his collarbone, eyes closed as I breathe him in. It's all warmth and clean skin. It feels like home.

Ah, shit.

Eyes flying open as realization crashes over me, I pull away from Cross like I've been shocked.

I stare at his sleep-relaxed face, the softened line of his jaw, the barely visible creases at the corners of his eyes, his mouth. I know the planes of his face, know how they change with sleep, anger, joy. Somehow, I've quietly catalogued each expression and locked that knowledge deep within my heart.

I'm in love with him.

Fuck.

Fuck.

I get out of bed carefully, doing my best to not wake him even as I panic. Slipping from his bedroom, I hurry to the kitchen and lean on the counter, breathing in through my nose and out through my mouth to try to steady my heartbeat. I don't bother turning on the lights. It's better in the darkness where no one can see me losing my damned mind.

How could I be so stupid? How in the hell did I manage to fling myself headfirst into... *feelings* without realizing it? Cursing, I pace across the cool tiles. It would be bad enough if we were just partners, but throw all of the supernatural crap in with it, and it's probably the worst mistake I've ever made in my life. Worse than when I was nearly killed during my first Burning, worse than finding Emma in a warehouse and vowing to avenge her death.

You okay? Priya asks, startling me enough that I jump.

No. I run my fingers through my hair and press the heels of my palms into my eyes. *No, I'm not okay.*

We'll figure out how to help him, she says softly. I want to laugh.

It's not that. I mean, it's not just *that.*

I lean my hip against the counter, and she settles next to me. Her body is cool and weightless against mine, and I shiver. *Do you want to tell me what's going on, or should I start guessing?*

I don't think it'll take you that long to get it.

Ah, you finally figured out that you love him.

I groan. *I hate you so much right now.*

No, you don't, she says. Her laughter isn't unkind, but I still crumple in the face of it. *Oh, Kim. Honey. Don't look like that. It's not a bad thing.*

I would beg to differ. I tip my head back and stare at the ceiling. *I'm such an idiot.*

You know he cares about you, too.

Not the problem, Priya. I fling myself away from her and start pacing again. *He might feel that way now, but he's not going to forgive me for what I did to him, not when he finds out. And what if we can't stop it? What if it*—my Sending cuts off with the force of my fear. I push, forcing myself to finish the thought. *What if it kills him?*

Kim.

It's unforgivable, what I've done to him. Tears prick my eyes. *I can't forgive myself for it.*

Her hand is cool on my hair. *Your forgiveness isn't the important thing here.*

I can't tell him, not now.

Then I think we both know how this is going to end, whether he gets better or not. If you can't talk to him about this, when it's this important...

I know. I curse. *I know. But how do you tell someone that they're dying, Priya? That it's your fault?*

She hushes me, Sending slow tendrils of comfort and understanding down our bond. I let her wrap me in her arms, let the tangle of her hair wrap around us. There's no real pressure to her touch, just a sense of coolness and the trickle of a soft breeze against my skin, but it's enough. I know she's there.

Her grip tightens, and I smell soot. *I won't let anything happen to you. You've suffered enough. Trust me to take care of you, to take care of this.*

My heart starts pounding.

Don't worry anymore, she whispers. Her breath smells like ash and blood. *I won't let anyone hurt you again.*

It hurts to drag the blue-white power into my body, to send it flowing out of me in a wave that crashes into

Priya's body and engulfs her in power. Screaming, she struggles against it, and I feel every push and pull like a punch to the gut. Her eyes, when she raises her head to snarl at me, are black.

Her arms blister and blacken. Thorny vines wrap their way around her hands, digging into her skin and leaving it cracked and bleeding.

Priya, I beg quietly, pouring more power into the binding, into our bond. *Priya, you've got to snap out of it.*

He won't have you, she says, mouth twisted into a sickening snarl. *No one will have you. You're mine.*

I shut my eyes, grit my teeth, and push. She screams, and the lamp on the desk rattles with it. Silently begging that she'll come back, I Send memories of us together through the bond. Our early days as partners, when we were still figuring each other out. The cautious friendship that built between us with time, that turned from grudging respect into deep-seated admiration and love. So much love, it's nearly overwhelming now. It chokes me, drags tears to my eyes, makes me clench my hands so hard that my nails bite through skin and drip blood onto the floor. I'm awash with it, pouring every ounce of it down our bond, hoping that it'll be enough to get her to stop, to drag her back from Turning.

Kim, she gasps, her voice filled with pain and confusion. *Kim, what's happening?*

I open my eyes, and she stares at me, her gray-white eyes wide and frightened.

You're Turning, I Send, grief-stricken. And somehow I know that's my fault, too.

I feel a headache building before the sun's even up. Groggily, I brew a pot of coffee and wait for Cross to join me in the kitchen. He stumbles from the bedroom about halfway through the brew cycle, his eyes red-rimmed and heavy-lidded.

"How're you feeling?"

He pulls a mug out of a cabinet, pushes in close to me so that he can grab the coffee carafe before it's even full, and pours himself a cup. Coffee trickles from the maker, sizzling on the heating element for a moment before he slips the carafe back in place. The smell of burning coffee fills the kitchen, but if it bothers him, I can't tell. He's too busy burying his nose in his mug, eyes closed as he takes a careful, too-long sip.

"Better than I have been, but I slept like shit." He opens his eyes, and they're black.

I'm frozen through in an instant. All I can do is stare in horror at the oil-slick sheen of his eyes. He frowns, then blinks, and when his eyes open, they're green and confused.

"You okay?"

"Yeah." It comes out as a whisper. "Just… I didn't sleep well, either."

"Sorry if I kept you up." He takes another sip and leans a hip on the counter. "I move around a lot when I can't sleep."

"It's fine." I can't breathe. "I barely noticed."

"That's good, then. So, what're your plans for

today?"

I mumble something about grabbing paperwork from HQ, getting my cases in order while I'm benched, but none of it sticks in my mind. There's a low buzz that I can't shake, a sound that grows louder as I stand in Cross's kitchen.

"I guess I'll get out of your hair, then." He finishes his coffee and yawns. "I'll text you later?"

I nod, then try to act normal when he brushes a kiss against the top of my head before wandering back to the bedroom. As soon as he leaves, though, I shudder out a breath and collapse against the counter.

Please tell me you saw that, I Send to Priya, doing my best to keep the panic from our bond and my voice.

See what?

When he... No, I must be imagining things. *Never mind.*

Cross comes out of the bedroom a few minutes later. He looks a little tired, but other than that, there doesn't seem to be anything wrong with him. When he pulls me close for a goodbye kiss, the press of his chest against mine burns.

"I'll see you later?" he asks against my mouth, and I nod. Our foreheads brush before our lips do, and then he's pushing me out the door with a soft smile.

My heart feels like it's breaking.

Paperwork? Priya asks, giving me a long look. *What are we really doing today?*

Keys in hand, I pick up my pace as I head to the

stairs.

We're going to see Taka.

For the first second after he opens the door, Taka looks surprised. It doesn't take him long to cover it, though, a familiar placidity smoothing over his face.

"Kim. Thank you for dropping by. I was going to call you later today."

I make some kind of affirmative noise before stepping inside. Habit has me toeing off my shoes before I can tell him I won't be staying long.

"Let me make some tea," he says after shutting the door. He walks quietly into the kitchen, and the everyday sound of the tea kettle banging into the faucet as he fills it makes me want to forget my anger.

As I settle at the low table, Claire appears nearby.

He's been upset, she Sends to me, her hair floating about her head in an uneasy cloud.

So have I.

You could at least talk to him civilly. Courtesy is the least you owe him.

I turn away from her, trying to ignore the stinging truth of her words. Taka comes out of the kitchen before I'm forced to respond, a tea tray in hand. The scent of *genmaicha* drifts up from the cup as he pours it for me. I cradle its warmth and calming scent in my hands as he takes a seat.

"Might I ask what prompted this visit?" he asks,

taking his own cup in hand.

I wait as he takes a sip, drawing out the pause in conversation until it's razor thin and just as cutting. His expression doesn't change much, only a slight wrinkling at the corners of his eyes, but I can read the pain there. It's enough.

"I'm hoping you have information for me," I say at last. "About what Ruth's doing."

His mouth twists into an unhappy frown. "I do, though I am afraid the conversation did not go as well as I had hoped it would."

"Well? What've you got?"

He puts his tea down on the table and holds it between his fingers. "It was difficult to ask questions without giving away any details, but I assumed that you wanted anonymity. I was unable to learn more about your additional Affinities, but she did tell me more about the markers." He looks up. "They have plans to put up more."

"What? Why?"

"The ones they have in place do not appear to be collecting power as well as they had previously. It's overflowing and gathering in new places."

I take a sip of tea, thinking. *They've had those markers in place for decades*, I Send to Priya. *Why would their system start failing now?*

There've been more Turned ghosts lately, too, and we know from experience that the energy causes ghosts to Turn faster.

"The energy is increasing," I say quietly. "And they

can't control it."

"That was my thought, too."

"Did she say anything about why?"

He shakes his head. "They are as uncertain about the cause as we are. I will do what I can to find out more, but I am afraid that she has grown uncertain with my involvement in the group."

"What's that mean?"

He takes a long pause, drinking his tea and fighting to keep his expression steady. I can tell he's holding back anger, but why, I don't know.

"It means that she does not trust me as she once did," he says. "Something about my line of questioning has made her suspicious. Considering the strength of our friendship, I am... less than happy." Glancing at me quickly, he looks away again. "It is amazing what distrust can do to a relationship."

"Isn't it?"

"Kim..."

"Look, I get it." I spin the cup in my hands. "You thought you were doing the right thing, keeping it from me. But I'm not a kid anymore."

"You will always, in some ways, be a child to me, Kim. But you're right, I should not have assumed that you couldn't handle this information. I am doing what I can to make up for my mistake."

"I know." I feel chastised, though Taka's the one apologizing. "I just... The whole thing makes me so... I can't explain it."

"It is difficult to understand, and the possible repercussions are dangerous. I think I understand completely."

We fall into silence. There's only the sound of ceramic on wood and our careful sips of tea. When I finish my cup, I push it to the center of the table and stand.

"Before you go," Taka says, "how is your partner doing?"

"Priya?" She's relaxing in the corner, and her head tips up at her name. "She's fine."

"No, your partner with the police, Detective Cross. The last time I saw him, he was in the hospital."

I flush. "He's been discharged, and he's resting at home. They've put him on medical leave for a bit, but I think he'll be fine. Just needs to heal up."

"And his powers... How are those? When I was contacted by his Mentor, she hadn't heard from him."

I frown. "I didn't realize you two were in touch."

"She has my number. I was as surprised to hear from her as you appear to be by the news."

"Yeah." I swallow. "His powers are... fine. He's still figuring out how to control them, but that comes with time."

"Of course. Nothing unusual, then?"

I think of black eyes and dark energy seeping from a broken chest.

"No, nothing unusual."

I thought we were working on honesty, Priya says sharply.

Taka may be able to help.

We don't know enough about what's happening with Cross to talk to Taka about it. Not with his connection to Peterson's group.

Why does that matter?

They don't have any more control over that energy than we do, but they're putting their fingers into it anyway. All we're trying to do is stop it. They want to control it. I don't like how it feels.

Priya pauses. *You think they'd want to control Riley?*

Or experiment on him or something, I don't know. Whatever it is secret organizations do.

You've been watching too many sci-fi shows. She flicks her gaze to Taka, then back to me. *Okay. For now, we should keep it to ourselves. You're right. We don't know what their intentions are or what Taka might have to give up to get us more information. But,* she adds, her eyes narrowing, *I don't like it.*

"I appreciate you finding out what you can. If you learn anything else…"

"I will call you." He stands as I do, then follows me to the door. As I slip my shoes on, he takes my hand. His skin feels papery thin, and for the first time, I'm reminded of his age and mortality. "Please be safe, Kim."

"Yeah, I will." I squeeze his hand and let it drop. "I'll talk to you soon."

He holds the door open for me, and even though I hear it close a moment after I'm past the threshold, I know he watches me until I'm in my car and driving away.

CHAPTER NINE

A s I steer onto the highway, I pull Andrea's number up on my phone. Clicking it over to speaker, I listen to it ring. I'm getting nervous that it's going to flip over to her voice mail when she answers.

"Hey, Detective. To what do I owe the pleasure?"

"We've got a problem."

There's a long pause. "You want to elaborate on that, or just make me guess?"

"The binding. It's already failing?"

"Seriously?" She curses. "That didn't take long."

"You knew it was going to?"

"I *assumed* it would. Most bindings are temporary. I figured it would buy us some time to figure out what the real problem is."

"Well, it didn't buy us enough."

"Okay, okay, calm down." She huffs out a breath into the phone. "I've got some ideas for a stronger binding. Let me dig into that while you keep investigating where that shit's coming from."

"We're going to need it soon. Whatever that power

is, it's hurting Cross."

"Okay. Give me a couple of days to come up with something."

"I'm holding you to that, Andrea. I don't know what else we can do to help him right now."

"I'll call you, I promise. Be safe, Detective, and good luck."

"Thanks." I hang up and throw my phone into the cup holder.

You know it's only going to be a stopgap, Priya says quietly. *Whatever Andrea comes up with, it's not going to be enough.*

We'll figure it out before it becomes a problem. I'm not going to let that energy destroy him.

Then we'll to have to find a lead sooner rather than later. He's on borrowed time.

I don't have anything to say to that, and Priya doesn't have much to say the rest of the ride back to my apartment. I feel her watching me, though, like ants crawling across my skin. Occasionally, I catch the hint of wood smoke in the car, but when I turn to check, her hands are unblemished and resting gently in her lap.

As I park, she eases her way through the door and waits for me outside. The second my foot hits the pavement, she speaks.

I think we need to look at your grandmother's diaries again.

I lock the car and head inside. Priya floats behind me, near enough to my shoulder that I can feel the cool air that surrounds her.

I know they didn't tell us anything useful about Baker's Binding the last time we checked, but you can Read now, and you've had experience with getting memories out of someone's personal diaries. If you could do it with Comfort Bell's things, you can absolutely do it with your grandmother's.

My thighs are aching as I round the landing to the second floor. *I don't see what we'll gain from it.*

What we'll gain? Priya sounds astonished. *Kim, you'll be able to see inside your grandmother's mind. It'll be another perspective on the binding, one that comes from someone who was close with Baker before he was Bound, before he turned into whatever he is now. That's valuable insight into the enemy we're facing.*

We don't know that we're facing Baker, only that whatever he did to possess Cross likely caused this whole… situation to worsen.

Priya scoffs, and I start up the final flight of stairs to the apartment.

You and I both saw what happened when that Turned ghost went after Cooper, and if you think it was Riley running the show, I think you're painfully mistaken. Even Andrea thinks he was possessed.

My keys are tangled in the keyring, and it takes me a long minute to get them woven through so that they hang neatly from the metal loop. I grab the apartment key and jam it into the lock with more force than necessary. The door unlatches easily, and I push my way inside.

Priya's crossing the threshold when I close the door, and she glares at me as it passes through her.

If you're just afraid of what you might see—

Of course I'm afraid of what I might see. I throw my keys on the small side table and kick off my boots. *Christ, Priya, it's been weird enough Reading Comfort Bell's diary or Alvarez's notebook, and don't get me started on Jackie's death. What if…* I swallow. *I don't know, what if I find out she hated me or something? Or that she resented having to take me in?*

Oh, Kim. Priya's face falls. *Honey, that's not what you're going to see. She loved you.*

I know that, but you can love someone and still hate them a little.

She floats close and wraps her arms around me. *She loved you, and even if she did feel anything negative toward you, you're not going to be trying to Read the diaries from when you were alive, just from around the time of Baker's Binding. She didn't know you then. There won't be anything about you to find.*

I don't know why that thought stings, but it does. I'm not sure I want to think about my grandmother's life from before she was a grandmother. Hell, from before she was a *mother*. It's disconcerting to think of her as separate from her role in my life.

But Priya does have a point.

Do you really think I'll find anything?

I think it's better that you try and come up with nothing than leave a possible source unquestioned.

Okay, you have to stop watching procedurals. I look toward the backroom and wait for the knots in my stomach to come undone. *I'll try, but no promises.*

Her diaries are still a bit haphazardly stacked from

the last time I went through them. I grab the one with the missing section of pages, as well as the diaries from before and after. The three books feel heavier than they should. I'm weighed down by them as I walk back into the living room. I grab my knife from the side table and settle on the couch.

Spreading the three diaries out on the table in chronological order, I grab the middle one. Might as well start with the one I know should have something useful in it first.

I'm flipping through the entries from around the binding, looking for a potentially useful entry, when the back of my neck goes cold. The icy touch trails its way around the sides of my head, seeping into my scalp and temples. It coats my veins, fills my body with translucent ice, and encases me in shimmering, pearlescent pain.

Priya, I Send, but my voice sounds far away and muffled, even to my own ears. *Help*.

Whatever it is, it's too late. As quickly as the ice encases me, it cracks, and I'm stumbling without falling, tripping out of my body and into some kind of in-between state that I barely have time to recognize before the world around me collapses, condenses, shifts. As I fight for balance, images whip around me. There are faces, voices, all of them familiar but in an indistinct way. I know I should recognize them, but every time I try to see who's speaking, they slip out of focus. My stomach twists with nausea as I fight to find anything to hold on to.

"Joseph, it's a bad idea."

My grandmother solidifies in front of me. Everything around her is dark and faded. I don't know where she is or who she's talking to. I can tell that whatever I'm Seeing is in the past, though.

She's young. There are only the hints of wrinkles in the corners of her eyes, and her hair—white for as long as I knew her—is a rich blond, almost the same shade as my own. She tucks that hair behind her ear before crossing her arms.

"You've been over this time and time again, and I can't see it ending in any other way than badly."

"You don't understand."

A man walks into view. He's handsome, athletic. His black hair is closely cut but still thick, and his eyes are such a deep shade of brown, they almost look black.

"No, Joseph, I don't." My grandmother frowns.

"If you'd listen—"

"I've listened enough. Either you give this insane plan of yours up or we're through. I won't be a part of it."

He stills. His hands flex by his sides. "You don't mean that."

"I do." Her voice wavers. "I really do."

"Sadie, you can't—I need you."

"You need me to make it work." Even though her words are thick with tears, her voice is sharp as a blade. "That's all this ever was to you."

"That's not true."

"Does it matter if it is? I won't help you, Joseph. I won't."

The cold seeps in again, and my grandmother is whisked away into the swirling, shimmering black. I cry out, reaching for her, but it's too late.

I stumble back into myself, nearly falling off the couch as my apartment slips back into view around me. Gasping, I lean forward. Though I'm back from wherever the hell I went, my sense of balance is still twisting and twirling.

My stomach does not appreciate it.

I push myself to standing and weave my way toward the bathroom. My mouth fills with the taste of metal and saliva, and I've barely got the lid of the toilet pulled up and out of the way before I start heaving.

Bile stings the back of my throat and coats my tongue.

Are you all right? Priya's cool hands are frantic as they coast over my body. *What happened?*

I don't know. I groan and heave again. Spitting, I try to clear the taste from my mouth as I wait for the nausea to subside. Tears prick the corners of my eyes, and I wipe them away with a shaking hand. *I don't fucking know.*

Priya hovers as I slowly start feeling better. I flush the toilet and get back to my unsteady feet. Turning on the tap, I fill my hands with cold water and sip at it carefully. I rinse my mouth, spit, then do it again.

As I brush my teeth, I nearly gag, but the mint eases

some of the lingering sourness. When I spit this time, I'm not as worried that something else will come up with it.

You ready to talk to me now? Priya asks as I turn off the bathroom light and head back into the front room.

I fall onto the couch, pull the quilt down from the back of it, and groan into the cushions. *I think I saw the past.*

You Read it? Without blood?

I shake my head, though the motion is stilted by the cushion pushed against my cheek. *No, I don't think so. It didn't feel like that. Didn't look like it, either. Everything was shimmery and dark. It was… I don't know, it was weird as fuck.* Priya's silence lingers, and I crack an eye open to look at her. *You have any ideas?*

Not ones you're going to like.

I groan again. *Just rip the Band-Aid off, please.*

You've been able to Shake for, what, three days?

Give or take.

And what's changed since that started?

I frown. *Nothing?*

No. Riley's getting worse.

I roll onto my back and stare at her, not following.

Riley's getting worse, and there's more of that energy leaking from him. The energy that seems to determine whether or not a Medium will develop more than one Affinity.

Are you suggesting that because I've been with Cross basically this entire time, he's… what, given me another Affinity?

I think you Saw *the past, Kim. I think you're Seeing.*

Ah, fuck. I tug the blanket over my head and curse again. *I don't want to See the past.*

Better than Seeing the future, she says. *At least you know what happened, happened. You're not guessing at what could be.*

At least we'd have an idea of what's coming, I grouse. *Right now, I'd give anything to get a hint of where this is going to end up.*

That's not how Seeing works. The future isn't set in stone.

Tell that to all those rich yahoos who're paying Peterson to give them stock tips.

I'd kick you if I were corporeal, she says with a sigh. *Say you See Riley getting hit by a car while crossing the street. When the time comes, you do the right thing and stop him from crossing the street. Only problem is that now the driver isn't paying attention to the road, and they run a red light just as a school bus is going through the intersection.*

I get it, you don't have to kill a theoretical bus full of children to prove your point.

She settles next to me, and I shiver under the blanket at her cold touch. *The point is that when you See something in the future, you can change it, but not always for the better. At least when you look back, you know it's over and done with. That's all I'm saying.*

I pull the blanket closer around my shoulders. *Whatever I saw, I didn't learn anything new from it.*

I tell her about the vision, not that it takes long, and by the time I'm done, Priya's floating back and forth across the room, a ghostly approximation of pacing that I follow with half-lidded eyes.

Whatever Baker was planning, it was bad enough that your grandmother not only wouldn't help him with it, she went to an authority figure in the community about it.

And broke up with him, I add. *At least we're certain they were together now.*

Priya shakes her head. *How awful for Sadie.*

Yeah, it's always a bummer when you find out your boyfriend has been busy diabolically plotting behind your back. You'd think he would've had the decency to just cheat on her.

Priya ignores me. *We're no closer to figuring out what it is that Baker was trying to do, though. Or what he could be trying to do now.*

He was obsessed with power. Do you remember when we fought him in Elgin? It's all he kept talking about. I close my eyes, trying to remember. *And Moore, she said that Baker couldn't be trusted with that power.*

You think it's the same power that they're collecting at those markers? What's coming out of Cross?

Throat too tight to speak, I nod.

But… Priya hesitates. *I don't get it. That power is leaking out of Death, and that's where Baker is. He should be swimming in it. Why's he still going after power that he already has?*

Maybe he's still Bound?

Priya stops pacing and stares at me, wide-eyed. *I didn't think it would follow him into Death. That's… That's awful.*

No wonder they got rid of that book. I sit up with a groan. *No Medium in their right mind would want to have their abilities tied down for the rest of their afterlife, which there apparently is.*

There must be something, if Baker's still there.

I always wondered…

About what happened to ghosts?

I nod. *And people, Mediums. I just assumed it all… ended, but I guess not.* I take a breath, worry creeping in. *What do you think it's like? I mean, do Turned ghosts stop Turning, or do they just keep getting worse?*

I don't want to consider it. Priya shivers, her hair fanning out around her with the movement. *In the few moments when it's happened, it's… unpleasant. Imagining an eternity like that?*

I rub my eyes and throw the blanket to the side. My grandmother's diaries sit on the table, my knife waiting next to them.

I've gotta know.

I reach for the blade, dig the tip of it into my finger, and watch as blood beads against silver.

It smears across the cover, and then I'm gone.

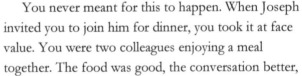

You never meant for this to happen. When Joseph invited you to join him for dinner, you took it at face value. You were two colleagues enjoying a meal together. The food was good, the conversation better, and you chalked it up to a lovely, spur-of-the-moment evening.

You didn't expect him to ask you again, or to say yes.

You didn't expect to like him so much.

Now, though. Now, you aren't so sure.

You've been to this diner before. It's not far from your apartment, and the coffee is good, which is why you told Caroline to meet you here. For the first time since you met her, though, she's running late.

Your diary is heavy beneath your hands, the leather smooth and even. It's a new journal, only the first handful of pages covered in your messy scrawl. Nervous, you run your thumbnail along the edges of the cover, finding comfort in the way the soft leather gives. You know the motion will wear the edge smooth over time. You've done this before.

Caroline slides into the booth across from you, and though you know you shouldn't, you flinch. There's something about her that leaves you off-balance, something about the pure strength in her every motion that makes you uncomfortable. You're strong enough in your own right, but she could throw you across the room without breaking a sweat, and that makes you distrustful of her.

Not to mention the way her eyes gleam whenever she talks about the future and what she sees coming for future generations.

"Sadie," she says, her voice worn smooth with age, "thank you for meeting with me. I know it's a bit of an imposition."

"It's fine." You move your hands from your journal to your coffee mug. You hold on. "What did you want to talk to me about? You weren't very specific on the phone, only that it had to do with Joseph."

"I didn't want to risk someone listening in. They're phasing out those party lines, but you never know who still has them."

You know that you don't, but you don't say anything about it. "Still, I'd like to know what all the secrecy's about."

"Yes, well. I'm not sure if you're aware, but Joseph has started doing some research lately."

You nod. The last time you went to his apartment, you noticed the piles of papers and books littering his kitchen table. He rushed you out the door before you were able to get a closer look, and, to be honest, it didn't strike you as odd at the time. Now, though, with one of the most powerful Mediums in the movement for Medium recognition sitting across from you in a rundown diner, you wish you did.

"Has he told you about it at all?" She doesn't wait for you to respond. "No, I can tell from your expression that he hasn't. Well, if you must know, it's a bit… esoteric. A bit *dangerous*, if I might be so bold as to say so. I have it on good authority that he's looking into… Well, he's looking into Death."

You raise your cup to your lips and burn your tongue as you take a long sip. When the sting resides, you answer, "Aren't we all?"

She laughs, though you didn't make a joke. "Not quite like that, I'm afraid." When she leans in, her eyes are bright and fervent. "I'd like you to keep an open mind."

She starts talking.

You start to listen.

I fall out of the Reading with a sickening lurch and let out a string of curses.

You okay?

Yeah, I grouse, throwing the diary onto the coffee table. It bumps against the other two volumes, then stops. *The damned memory cut off before I could learn anything useful.*

You could try to Read it again.

And we both know how successful that's been in the past. I rest my elbows on my knees, then my head in my hands. A moment later, I run my fingers through my hair, sighing. *I might not have seen anything useful, but I have an idea of when it occurred. It was dark out, but it wasn't that late, maybe 7:30, 8:00 p.m. Sadie was wearing a sweater, nothing too heavy but still warm.*

So either late spring or early fall.

I try to remember what I could see out the diner windows. *Spring, I think. There weren't any leaves on the trees, but there weren't any on the ground either. And it was before Baker was Bound, so that gives us a general year. If I look through the diary, I should be able to roughly place it.*

Priya smiles. *It's a start.*

Yeah. I lean back and yawn. *What time is it?*

Late enough that if you wanted to go to bed, no one would judge you for it.

I pull out my phone and check the time. There's a

text message from Cross from two hours ago waiting, the notification like a judgment on my screen.

Turning in early. See you in the morning?

Guilt swells, and I quickly text that I'll call him tomorrow. I don't expect a response, considering how long it's been since he texted, but I stare at my phone for a while after sending my message. Thumb tracing the edges of the phone, I wonder how he's feeling, how the binding is holding up.

I get ready for bed and fall into it gratefully. Though I miss the comforting weight of Cross's body next to mine—it's been a few weeks since we've slept apart, though we keep switching between our apartments—it's nice to not be on guard against the energy seeping from his chest. There's guilt mixed in with the relief, since it's all my own fault, but as I curl up in my bed and start to drift, I can't help but feel more comfortable than I have in days.

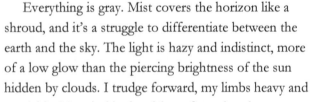

Everything is gray. Mist covers the horizon like a shroud, and it's a struggle to differentiate between the earth and the sky. The light is hazy and indistinct, more of a low glow than the piercing brightness of the sun hidden by clouds. I trudge forward, my limbs heavy and unwieldy. My mind is sluggish, as fogged as the landscape around me.

Dark smudges appear in the distance. They move in an unseen wind, bending and swaying like grass in a field. My skin prickles. The hair on the back of my neck stands up.

I keep walking toward them, whatever instinct is telling me to run muffled by the fog.

The shapes are larger than I first thought. As I draw closer, they loom higher and higher against the pale sky, barely visible but somehow more ominous for their indistinctness. It's not until I'm nearly at the foot of one that I realize what I'm looking at.

A corpse towers over me. It's arms and legs are bloated and blackened with decaying blood. Its stomach has already given way to the gasses building within it. Viscera swing from its gaping stomach and ribs; long loops of intestine, like the remnants of ragged clothes around its waist and hips, drag on the ground behind it. Its face, sunken and skeletal, turns slowly to look at me. Its mouth hangs open, its lower jaw held onto its skull by flimsy strips of skin and decayed muscle. The tongue lolls from the bottom of its jaw, the muscle a darkness in the shadow of its skull.

Burner, it whispers in my mind. One of its hands lifts sluggishly. It's massive, twice as big as I am even without flesh clinging to the bones. I stumble back, and the bones dig into the ground before me. The skeletal hand rests there for a moment and drags back toward the corpse. Its fingertips leave deep furrows in the ground that remind me of a field tilled for harvest.

More voices join the first, all of them whispering, *Burner, Burner, Burner* into my mind. I spin around, though even that terrified motion is slow. The air sticks to my skin and clothes. It grabs at me, and I drag power into my body before sending it out in a wave of blue-white and orange light.

The corpse stumbles back, and from the depth of its eye sockets, a red ember begins to burn.

Keeper, it whispers, and the other voices fall silent. They stare at me with sightless eyes, their bodies preternaturally still. The air around me feels like a held breath, the world poised and waiting.

Keeper.

It reaches for me again.

I bolt awake, panting, my body covered in sweat. Light glances through the window onto my dresser where Priya is sitting.

Watching.

Her eyes are shadowed, dark like the hollows of a skull.

It's okay, Kim, she Sends quietly. *Go back to sleep. I'll keep watch.*

It's a long time before I find sleep again.

Chapter Ten

I 'm in the kitchen making coffee when Taka calls me in the morning.

"Ruth wants to see you," he says as soon as I answer.

"Of course she does. Did she say why?"

"No." He sounds displeased. "She said that it was a matter between the two of you, and that I should try not to get involved any further."

"She sounds like such a lovely woman," I say as I start the coffee maker. "I can understand why you've been friends for so long."

"While your sarcasm is not appreciated, she was rather insistent on you meeting with her."

I shake my head, though he can't see it. "Not going to happen. Not unless she's ready to tell me about whatever it is they're trying to do with those markers."

Something whistles in the background and ceramic clinks nearby. "I don't know what she will or won't tell you, Kim. Perhaps sitting down to talk will help. It will at least allow you to ask your questions directly, rather than through me."

"Getting tired of playing telephone?"

"Yes."

I sigh. "I don't trust her, Taka. I don't know what she wants with me, or if whatever she's doing with that power is aboveboard. Hell, for all I know, she and her friends are making it worse."

"I do not think that she would try to harm anyone."

"And I'm not so sure." I pour coffee into my mug, then take a sip. "I mean, what kind of trustworthy person runs a secret organization? When has that ever been the plot twist in a movie?"

"I don't believe she means you any harm," he says, annoyance heavy in his voice. "She just wants to talk."

"I've heard that before." As he sighs down the line, I continue, "If you think it'll help, then I'll give her a call. But I'm not meeting up with her. If all she wants is to talk, she can do it over the phone."

"That's reasonable, though I doubt she'll be happy with it."

"Tough shit." I open a drawer and pull out a notepad and pen. "You got a number for me?"

He rattles it off, and I hurriedly write it down. After reading it back to him, I cap the pen and chuck it into the still-open drawer.

"I'll call her later this morning."

"I don't think you should delay this any further," he warns. "Ruth is not someone you want to make into an enemy."

"I'm not looking to make an enemy out of anyone."

"Still, be careful."

"I got it. No funny shit."

"Language."

For a second, it feels like we're back to normal. I languish in it, let the comfort of rote behavior sweep over me. My mouth twitches into a smile.

"I apologize," he says, breaking the moment like a guitar string snapping. Everything goes discordant inside of me. "I shouldn't speak to you like a child. Please let me know what more you learn or if you need anything else."

"Yeah, will do."

"Goodbye, Kim."

"Bye, Taka," I say, but he's already hung up.

I set my phone down on the counter next to the notepad. My coffee, gone slightly cold, is flat and bitter on my tongue. As I stare into the dark liquid, Priya comes closer and hovers her fingers over my shoulders and back.

That seemed to go well, she says, tone hopeful and full of forced cheerfulness.

I do my best to ignore the tension building between my shoulders. *I'm going to get a shower. After that, I'll check in with Cross.*

And Peterson?

Don't worry, I say as I leave my coffee, phone, and the notepad in the kitchen. *She's next.*

The pounding water and heat relax me enough that when I call Cross, I sound normal.

"How're you feeling?" I ask as I sit at the foot of my bed, my wet hair dripping down the back of my neck.

"Bit better," he says, though he doesn't sound it. "I slept like the dead last night. As soon as my head hit the pillow, I was out. How about you?"

"I slept okay. Had some weird dreams, though."

He pauses. "You want to talk about it?"

"Not really, no. It's strange, but I don't remember the details, only that they were upsetting."

"It's probably stress." I can hear the smile in his voice. "Not like you've got anything to be stressing about right now."

"No, nothing comes to mind. It's all roses and champagne over here."

He laughs. "Just make sure you save some for me."

"You think I'm going to share?"

"I'll make it worth your while."

I can't stop the grin from spreading across my face. "Detective Cross, I would never."

"I know for a fact you would." He yawns, and the warmth in my chest fades. "Christ, you'd think after all that sleep, I'd be awake by now."

"You're still recovering. Take it easy. Don't be too hard on yourself."

He scoffs. "You had a concussion and were trapped in a collapsed building for ten hours, and you seem to be doing fine."

"It's the Healing," I hedge. "It's giving me a boost."

"Well, next time I see you, why don't you boost me a bit? I'd love to feel a bit closer to human rather than comatose."

"I'll see what I can do." I glance at my alarm clock. "You want me to come over tonight?"

"If you want to, yeah. It's not like I've got any plans."

"You're in luck, then, because I don't either."

He laughs again, but it sounds less bright, more forced. "Then I'll see you tonight."

"Tonight, then. Go get some rest. You sound like you need it."

He groans. "I'm going to become one with the couch at this rate."

"At least I'll know where to find you."

"Fair enough." He yawns again. "I'll see you later."

"Bye."

I stare at my phone for a beat before hanging up, then curse. His continued exhaustion isn't a good sign for how well the binding is holding up, though I won't know the full extent of things until I see him later today. I stand and walk into the kitchen, forcing myself to keep an even, steady pace. Running to call Peterson won't make his situation any better or worse, and the last thing I want is to have her answer the phone with me out of breath from sprinting into the kitchen.

I dial her number and wait as it rings. Expecting a secretary or assistant to answer, I'm surprised when

Peterson's voice comes down the line.

"This is Ruth Peterson. To whom am I speaking?"

"It's Detective Kim Phillips. Taka gave me your number."

"I knew you were going to call, although I wasn't sure about precisely when." There's a smugness to her tone that grates on me immediately. "It's always hard to pin down the exact hour, especially when it's midday. I'm glad you called, though. I did have a few visions where you didn't."

"What do you want?"

"There's no need to be hostile, Detective." She sounds offended. "I do remember how kind you were when Emma... Well, I think it doesn't need to be said that I would like to return the favor of your kindness, if you'd let me."

"Then tell me what in the hell your organization is doing. What's going on with those markers? Why are you trying to control that power?"

She sighs. "You don't believe in hedging your bets, do you?"

"I want to know the truth." I start pacing. "I want to know that I can trust you."

"I would think that the latter would precede the former. How can you know that what I tell you is the truth if you don't trust me first?"

My head pounds. "Look, just answer my questions."

"Fine." Papers shuffle in the background. "As I'm sure you're aware, there is a powerful energy running through the world. It ebbs and flows, like most things do, and in the places where it gathers, things congregate that would abuse that power. The markers are meant to dissipate that energy, to spread it more evenly across Chicago so that there aren't any great wellsprings for ghosts to drink and Turn from."

"Is that why you have dead Mediums watching them? To deal with any Turned ghosts that might show up?"

"So you have done your research. Taka warned me that you were thorough." She sighs. "Yes, that is part of it, though it's not a precise science. For one thing, it was difficult to convince the ghosts of Mundane people to guard the power. For another, they were more susceptible to the pull of it."

I exhale. "They Turned, too."

"More or less."

"What's that supposed to mean?"

For the first time, her confident tone wavers. "It doesn't really matter what it means."

"I think it does."

"Then that's the easiest way to explain it, yes. They Turned, in a way, after prolonged exposure to the energy."

I think of Rivera, of White, of the man at the first marker. All of them Turned, but all of them Turned unlike any other ghosts I'd encountered up to that point. All were surrounded by dark energy and feeding off of it.

"I think I understand," I say. "You're still gathering that energy, though. It's still collecting in places and drawing ghosts to it."

"But it's not where it wants to be or as densely packed as it would be otherwise," she says like she's speaking to an infant. "If we were to let it run free, the consequences would be dire."

"Yeah, I bet they would be."

"If you don't want to listen to what I have to say, then I don't see the point of continuing this conversation."

"I want you to tell me what the fuck is going on in my city," I snap.

"Nothing is going on in your city, Detective. We have everything under control."

I laugh. "Yeah, it certainly seems like you do."

"Do you have any other questions, or are we done?"

"What are you going to do about the ghosts, the ones being drawn to it?"

"We're handling it. There are multiple Burners in the organization and they are more than capable of managing a handful of spirits."

"Of course." I want to hit something. "You've got your finger in the dike, and you're hoping the water doesn't get any higher."

"That's a gross distortion of the truth, Detective. There's nothing to be concerned about. We've got it handled."

"I'll remember that the next time a building-sized

ghost tries to murder someone. You have a good day, Ms. Peterson."

I hang up, fuming.

I'm always impressed with your people skills, Priya says. *Fine form today, Kim.*

I turn toward her, suddenly exhausted. *Can you not right now? They're fucking things up, and it's affecting you as much as it's affecting me and Cross, not to mention all the other ghosts in Chicago. If that shit's making* you *Turn, what does that mean for the unbonded ghosts who are waiting to either pass on or be Burnt? What's that mean for all the people who might come into contact with them?* I scrub my hand over my face. *They're fooling themselves if they think they have this situation under control.*

Then we need to figure out where this extra energy is coming from and figure out how to stop it.

Mediums have known about this energy for forever, I say, looking around the apartment for my keys. *There's got to be some kind of information about it at the Newberry, right? Someone has to have looked into it by now.*

You want to go do research? She sounds surprised.

I want to get to the bottom of this. If that means some time spent in the stacks, then let's go.

⸻

The Victoria Carter Memorial Library is relatively empty when I walk through its front doors. There's a feeling of calm silence hanging about the place that makes some of the tension in my shoulders fade.

The librarian supervising the information desk looks

up from her computer screen as I walk up to her desk, a polite smile spread across her face.

"How can I help you today?"

"Hi, I'm looking for anything you might have on the power that Mediums use. Anything at all."

She frowns. "You mean like explaining the difference between a Burner and a Shaker? We have quite a few books on the different Affinities and how they work."

"No, not that." I frown, trying to think of how to explain it. "There's power all over the place, and Mediums tap into it, right? I'm wondering if you have any resources on the power itself, rather than on how Mediums use it."

Her eyebrows rise. "I don't think I've heard of anything like that. Let me check the catalogue. One moment."

She types on her computer and scrolls through whatever results have come up. The furrow between her brows deepens. A moment later, she's angrily backspacing, then typing again. And again. The cycle repeats a few more times before she lets out an annoyed breath.

"I'm not finding anything that fits exactly what you're looking for, but there's a research paper from a few years ago that might have something useful. Worst-case scenario, you can always check the bibliography for other resources."

It's better than nothing.

"That'll work."

"Okay, give me a minute to get you settled."

She writes something on a slip of paper, stands, and walks over to a bank of computers, waving at me to follow. I trail after her and wait patiently as she logs into the terminal. After pulling up a website, she types something in. As soon as the page loads, she steps back.

"There you go. It's online only, sorry."

"Not a problem. Thank you for your help."

She smiles again and heads back to the information desk. Slipping into the chair, I lean forward and read.

A lot of the article sounds like what Dave told us a few days before, but it argues that while there are natural phenomena that control and manage the energy coming from Death—chalk, silver, water—those elements don't account for all of that energy's behavior.

Look at the Dover Cliffs, the article says. *They are primarily composed of chalk, which would lead one to assume that there would be little to no supernatural activity in this area. However, there are large stores of energy all along the coastline, and many ghosts of suicide victims Turn relatively quickly at the Cliffs. If the presence of chalk were the only limiting factor on whether or not ghosts would present in an area, then what is seen at Dover is impossible. There must be other factors at play, ones that aren't readily apparent to the living.*

I lean back in my chair, dissatisfied and annoyed. Before I leave, I print the article. The pages are still warm when I pull them from the printer.

The trip downtown's been a waste of time, and as I

weave my way through the crowded streets, I do my best to not lose the sense of urgency I felt after talking to Peterson earlier. Even though it wasn't productive, it gave me another avenue of investigation to pursue. It didn't pan out, but it's not the first time I've been on the trail of a suspect only to have to go in a different direction because of new evidence or witness statements. This is no different. I just have to figure out what my next lead is.

Or if there are any.

My phone rings, startling me out of my bad mood. I'm more than a little surprised to see Lieutenant Walker's name on the screen when I take it from my pocket. I duck into an alley, trying to get away from the noise of downtown as much as possible, and answer the phone.

"Lieutenant," I say as I continue walking. "How can I help you?"

"The IAB investigation has turned up a few questions about your investigation into Dominguez's murder. Specifically, that while you were working the case, you went to the morgue."

My gut clenches. "I did."

"And according to Dr. Abramo, you *bled* on the corpse?"

Ah, fuck.

"Yes, ma'am."

"Do you want to explain to me," she growls, "why my lead detective was contaminating evidence in the murder case of a confidential informant?"

There's a headache in my future, I can feel it.

"I was using my Medium abilities to find out more about the murder victim and his death."

"Of course you were." She sighs heavily into the phone. "There's a deposition scheduled for the week when you get back from leave. Expect to be there, Detective."

"Of course. Whatever IAB needs."

"And," she says, anger creeping into her voice, "if you're going to pull this shit again, you're going to get approval for it *before* you smear your goddamned DNA all over a murder victim, do you understand me?"

"Ma'am, I was—"

"I don't want to hear it, Phillips."

"Understood."

"Now," she says, her tone softening, "how's Detective Cross? I've tried calling to check in, but he hasn't answered."

"He's recovering," I say evasively, "but he's sleeping a lot. Maybe he missed your call."

"Tell him to give me a ring next time you see him."

"Of course." I want to ask why she wants to talk to him, but I keep my mouth shut instead. There's enough shit-stirring around. No need to make it any worse. "Is there anything else you need, Lieutenant?"

"No, not right now. I'll see you in a week, Phillips."

"See you then."

She hangs up before I can, and I slump against the

alley wall, my knees suddenly weak.

I didn't think about the implications of my blood on Dominguez's body—not in the context of the case at large. Christ, I probably made myself a person of interest in the damned IAB case by Reading his corpse. I shove my phone into my pocket and wait for the anger and self-recrimination to fade.

Unsurprisingly, they don't.

Still, there's a week left on our medical leave, and even knowing that my career might be in jeopardy, it seems like less of an immediate concern than Cross's failing health and the dark energy filling up the city. Knowing I'm not involved in the dirty cop ring eases my mind a bit, but knowing that I might be suspected of it… That stings.

I make my way back out of the alley and head to my car.

Don't worry, Priya says as we get in. *You documented what you were doing, even if you didn't specify why. They won't be able to say that you weren't doing your job appropriately.*

I'm not worried about that, I say, pulling into traffic. *I'm a good cop. They're not going to find anything that says otherwise.*

But?

But, I don't like the suspicion that I might not be.

I won't let them hurt you.

I roll my eyes. *They're not hurting me. It's not a big deal.*

You're upset, though.

I glance at her out of the corner of my eye, then still. Her hands are bloody and cracked open, the skin red and peeling away.

I make my voice as calm and even as possible. *It's okay, Priya. You don't have to be upset on my behalf.*

Clearly, I do. They don't respect you enough or what you do for them. They don't deserve you, don't appreciate you the way I do.

Priya, it's okay. Look at me. Her eyes are streaked with black like ink dropped in water. As she holds my gaze, the darkness fades, melting into the usual gray. She's the first to break eye contact. Staring at her hands, she freezes.

How long have they been like that? she asks in a whisper.

A few minutes at most. Not long.

Not long... She turns her palms up, then back down, and watches as the skin slowly knits back together. When the last of her wounds heals back over neatly, leaving no sign of injury behind, she clenches her fists and curses.

We'll figure it out, I say, though both of us know we have no idea why it's happening or how to stop it. *We'll just... We'll keep you away from Cross, make sure you aren't in close contact with him. Our bond's strong enough that you could stay in the hallway or a room over. We'll make it work.*

She's still staring at her hands. *I didn't feel it. I didn't even realize...*

It's okay.

Is it, though? She's somber, her expression unreadable. *I didn't know it was happening. What if I can't tell until it's too late, and I've done something to hurt you or Riley? This is bad,*

Kim. This is really bad.

And just like we'll figure out what's going on with Cross, we'll figure out what's going on with you. Peterson said that ghosts were susceptible to that energy. Maybe that's all this is.

And what? We get rid of it, and I go back to normal? We both know that once a ghost starts Turning, they don't stop.

But you're not just a ghost—you're bonded. Bonded ghosts don't Turn.

Except that we both know I am.

You aren't.

The car falls quiet, and as I note my speed, I ease off the accelerator. I didn't realize I'd started speeding.

It's got to be something else. I refuse to believe…

It doesn't matter what you believe. She sounds resigned, and it makes my chest ache. *It's what's happening.*

I push away the sting of her words. *Peterson's people figured out a way to stop the ghosts guarding the markers from Turning. We can, too.*

Okay, Kim. There's a quiet pulse of emotion across our bond, but I can't place what it is. It's indistinct but sits heavy in my gut all the same. *It can't hurt to try.*

I force optimism into my tone, though there's a ball of lead making its way through my gut. *Exactly. We'll figure it out.*

We don't talk the rest of the drive to Cross's apartment. The silence between us is unsteady and oppressive. I feel it like a heavy weight across my shoulders, pressing me deeper and deeper into the driver's seat. When I glance at Priya, she's looking out the window or at her hands, turning them over again and again.

I pretend I don't see her singed fingertips.

CHAPTER ELEVEN

I t takes a couple of presses on Cross's intercom before he answers.

"Who is it?" he asks, his voice distorted by the speaker.

"It's me. You want to let me in?"

The door buzzes open, and I hurry up to his apartment. The door's cracked open, and I push my way inside, frowning.

"What is it with people in my life wanting to get robbed?"

The empty front room doesn't answer, and I shut the door behind me and lock it like a sane person.

"Cross?" I toe off my shoes. "Where are you?"

"Bedroom."

I follow his voice and find him buried under the covers, the top of his head peeking out from the comforter. Sitting down on the edge of the mattress, I pull it down, feeling a painful mix of fondness and worry.

"You doing okay?"

"No."

He doesn't look like he is, either. His eyes are closed, and there are deep shadows beneath them that look like bruises against his unnaturally pale skin. His forehead is sticky with sweat when I push his hair back, but he doesn't feel feverish. A shudder works its way through his body, and he groans like the motion hurts.

With the blanket pulled back a bit, I can see the sheets stained with the red-black energy. It's pooled against his body, clinging to his chest and upper arms in patches. I must be getting used to the feel of it whenever I'm around him because there's only the slightest bit of a sting when my fingers accidentally brush it.

"How long have you been like this?"

"Dunno," he mumbles as he tugs the blankets back up around his chin. "Started around lunch."

I check the clock and wince. "That's a couple hours, Cross. Have you taken anything? Eaten? Drank?"

He groans. "No food, I'm too nauseous. But I took some Tylenol and had water."

There's an empty glass on the nightstand, and I grab it. "I'll get you some more."

My hand shakes when I refill the glass in the kitchen sink, and I set it down before I drop it. I put both hands on the counter and lean in, head tipped forward, as I breathe.

What do you want to do? Priya asks. Her arms are flushed, the tips of her fingers black. When I meet her eyes, the gray is stained with soot.

Andrea's binding started failing almost as soon as I put it in place, and it's only been getting worse. I know she said she was going to call when she had something, but it can't wait.

I fumble for Andrea's number and wait as it rings.

"Detective." Her voice is steady, though I feel anything but. "You need the binding."

"I need the binding."

"You're lucky I had some PTO to burn." There's rustling in the background, like pieces of paper being shuffled across a tabletop. "I've been working on it since you and I last talked, and I had to call in some *really* big favors, but I think I've got everything you need to make this work. It's more complicated than the last one—I'm sure that comes as a complete shock to you—so I'm going to send you the diagrams and some supplemental materials." I open my mouth to speak, but she cuts me off before I can. "I *know* you don't have time to read, but you *have* to go over this or it's not going to work. This binding isn't like the last one. You can't just scribble on his chest and call it a day. You're going to have to encase him in a circle, and it has to be *perfect* or it's not going to hold."

"How long will it last?"

"That all depends on how good of a job you do when you draw it out. Any line out of place, even slightly, is going to impact its longevity. If you do it exactly right and that energy doesn't keep increasing, you'll get a month, maybe two."

Relief sweeps through me like a clean breeze. "I don't know how I can thank you."

"Keep that cute partner of yours out of trouble, and next time you see me, you can buy me a coffee."

"It's a date. And thank you again."

I hang up and stare at my phone until a message from Andrea comes through. There are a handful of images attached, along with a link to an online document. I open all of them and review them until my eyes start to hurt from staring at the screen. I blink until the afterimage of my phone fades and rub my eyes.

Andrea wasn't kidding when she said it was complex. Running through the runes and sigils in my mind and the intricate lines connecting it all together, I wonder how the fuck I'm going to scribe the damned thing without Cross catching on.

And I'm going to need a hell of a lot more chalk.

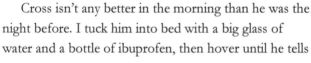

Cross isn't any better in the morning than he was the night before. I tuck him into bed with a big glass of water and a bottle of ibuprofen, then hover until he tells me to go away.

"I'm fine, Kim," he says, looking anything but. "Just... go do something somewhere else. I don't need you watching me sleep."

"You're sure?"

He glares at me, though the effect is dimmed a little when he has to fight a yawn. "Yes. Now, go away."

He throws the blanket over his head, and my heart twinges with affection and fear. God, I love him and it's awful.

I review Andrea's binding again, if only to confirm my thought from the night before that I'll need more supplies. I text Taka that I'm on my way over and head out.

"Make sure you stay hydrated!" I shout to Cross. There's no reply and I hope he's getting some rest. Locking the door, I step into the hallway and let it fall shut behind me.

The drive to Taka's is mindless and does little to settle my nerves. Even the traffic isn't enough to distract me.

Priya seems to understand that I need the quiet and remains silent. Instead, she sits in the passenger seat and Sends quiet and calm down our bond. There are brief snaps of worry, of fear, but they're quickly overwhelmed by the love she pours after.

Her hands are pale and steady as they rest in her lap, no sign of burns anywhere on her arms. It adds to my relief, though I briefly wonder if I should say something to Taka. He's been a Burner for longer than I've been alive. It's a slim hope, but if he's ever heard of it, maybe he'll know how to stop it.

By the time I pull up outside Taka's house, I feel better.

That is, until I note the unfamiliar SUV in his driveway.

The black Range Rover, with its tinted windows and chrome rims, screams money and prestige, and the inch-and-a-half-thick glass says whoever is sitting inside needs protection.

Considering the people Taka knows who might need a car like this, I don't have to be a Seer to guess who's waiting inside.

I knock on the door and wait until Taka opens it, his mouth twisted into an unhappy frown.

"Kim. Right on time."

"I guess." He steps back and gestures for me to come in. I toe off my boots when there's a quiet cough from the direction of the kitchen.

Turning my head, I find Ruth Peterson seated at Taka's low table. Her hair is in a tidy bun, and she's wearing a light gray pantsuit that looks like it costs more than a car payment. She's incongruous in the middle of Taka's house, as if sitting on the floor while wearing Chanel somehow makes the fashionable outfit cheap. She smiles tightly at me as I stare.

"Detective Phillips. A pleasure to see you."

"I can't say the same."

Taka frowns. "Your manners, Kim. Ruth is a guest in my house."

"I won't be staying long." I return her polite smile and turn to Taka. "I need chalk dust, and I'm nearly out. I'm hoping you've got some?"

"Of course." He gestures for me to sit across from Peterson. "I'll only be a moment."

I stay standing, arms crossed, while he wanders out of the front room and farther into the house. The silence that falls around Peterson and me is awkward and oppressive. She keeps giving me pointed looks that

I can't make heads or tails of. Eventually, I get tired of her staring at me and sit.

"Just tell me whatever it is you want to tell me so I can get out of here, okay? I'm not going to start a fight with you while we're in Taka's house."

"I don't want to fight with you, Detective. Or may I call you Kim?"

"No. Now, talk."

"You were, perhaps, more accurate in your assessment of the situation during our phone call the other day than I may have indicated." She shifts her weight, wincing with the motion. If she's been sitting there for long enough, her legs have probably fallen asleep. I take a bit of satisfaction in her discomfort. "We have been using the markers for generations to control and contain the energy moving through Chicago, but as of late, that has not been enough."

"So it *is* increasing."

She sniffs. "It's always increasing. It always will increase. That power is Death, and there will always be more dead. That's just the nature of things. But there is also more Life, usually in balance, and the two forces counteract each other. But not any longer, not in Chicago." Staring at me with that same pointed expression as before, she leans forward. "There is another source for the energy, one that we have yet to pinpoint, but do not doubt that we will. However, until that source is found and contained, the markers won't be enough to keep the power from gathering and letting the dead through."

"What?" I nearly choke on the word. "What do you mean, letting the dead through?"

"That power is Death in its most concentrated form. When it occurs in large enough amounts, the barrier between Life and Death is weakened, and Turned ghosts can come back through, into Life."

"How many of them?"

Peterson's expression doesn't change. "All of them."

I can't breathe. I reach out for Priya, searching for her through our bond. A moment later, she appears by my side, her hand on my shoulder. Her fingertips are stained black.

Don't worry, I won't let anything hurt you.

No one's trying to hurt me. I just... I need you.

Her hand flexes on my shoulder, though I can only see it, not feel it. A moment later, the black stain fades. *It's okay. I'm okay.*

Peterson, her eyes slightly unfocused, frowns. "I see it's already affecting your partner."

"What are you talking about?"

"The energy. It affects all ghosts, not just those that are unbound and waiting to move on. Even Bound ghosts aren't immune to it, though it has less of a pull on them than others." She raises an eyebrow. "She is Turning, correct?"

"No."

Yes. Priya moves away from me, closer to Peterson. *Though it comes and goes.*

"That is how it tends to happen." She gives Priya a

long, considering look. "You don't seem to be suffering much at the moment."

No, but like I said,—she glances at me—*it comes and goes.*

"It is possible to resist the pull. You've been to our markers, correct?" At my nod, she continues. "Then you've seen the ghosts guarding the pools. Some of them have been there for hundreds of years without any ill effect. I could, possibly, teach your partner here how to fight against it, to stop the Turning from getting any worse."

"And the catch?"

She smiles, and it's like staring down a criminal from across an interrogation table, like watching a predator that knows its prey is within striking distance.

"The source of the power. I've Seen that you'll find it. All I ask is that when you do, you call and tell me where it is. Simple, easy. If you agree, then my group will teach your partner what she needs to know to stop Turning. She likely won't need it, though, once we cut off the additional source."

"And if I don't?"

"Then you'll be wasting an opportunity. We will find where it's coming from, Kim. It's only a matter of time."

I open my mouth to respond, but Taka walks in carrying a large plastic container of chalk dust. He holds it out to me, waiting as I get to my unsteady feet.

My legs have fallen asleep.

I take the container with a murmured thanks and head to the door.

"Please let me know what you think, Detective," Peterson says from where she's still sitting at the table. "I hope to hear from you soon."

CHAPTER TWELVE

I cast the second binding on Cross two days later. I do my best to not hover during the day, and he does his best to not let on how annoying he finds it. We binge nature documentaries, and I pathologically check the failing runes and sigils on his chest while he falls asleep to the sound of David Attenborough talking about the rain forest.

Dinner is simple—pasta and canned sauce with a lackluster salad that barely deserves the name—and after nearly nodding off halfway through the meal, Cross turns in early, exhaustion weighing heavily on him. The symbol on his chest bleeds, leaving a trail of red energy throughout the apartment. I quietly Burn it behind him, letting my instincts snap out and send it hissing into nothingness. Priya judges me quietly from the edges of the room but doesn't dare come any closer to the energy than she already has, her eyes swirling with black and her skin bubbling when she draws too close.

I crawl into bed with Riley, letting him pull me into his arms while I do my best to not flinch away from the energy pouring from him. Thankfully, he falls asleep easily, and I pull away without disturbing him. Looking at him, asleep and face younger for it, I swallow against the rising tide of regret and self-recrimination I feel whenever I look at him.

It's my fault, but I'm trying my best to fix it. Andrea's binding nearly worked the first time. This new one has to. There's no other option.

Scribing the circle is hard to do in the dark and without waking Cross. I have to use chalk dust to account for the change in surfaces; it's the only way to keep the lines unbroken between the bed and the floor. Looking between Andrea's diagram and the room, I take my time laying it all out with careful precision. I double- and triple-check the runes and sigils, adjusting them minutely where the design is off, then step back and look at the whole thing spread around Cross's body.

Thank God the man's exhausted and a heavy sleeper.

What do you think? I Send to Priya, biting my lip as anxiety ripples through me. *You think it'll work?*

I think it would be better if you just told him, she says, annoyed, *but since you seem dead set against doing that, yes, it looks like this is a more precise binding than the last one. It's more targeted to the weakness in the symbol.*

Here's hoping it works. I take my knife out, but rather than pricking my thumb, I run the blade across my palm, cupping it as blood slowly fills it. Carefully, I turn my hand to the side and let the pooled blood spill onto the thick line of dust.

As the power wrenches its way from my body, I'm painfully reminded why I much prefer chalk sticks. The dust is thicker, heavier, and it takes so much more from me, a gutting sweep of energy that has me gasping and my legs going weak. I barely miss the brightly burning line of light as my knees hit the floor, my blood still dripping slow and steady from my hand. Once the light spreads from where I'm kneeling to fully encircle Cross's body, every chalk line lit up like the Fourth of July, I turn my hand palm up and trickle a bit of Healing into the wound. It stitches up with a fierce sting.

The binding around Cross glows brighter, lights branching up from the twisted symbols spread across the room. They meet above his body, tangling together in sweeping, elegant arches. Slowly, they settle over him, a net of woven light. They sink into his body, fading as they disappear beneath his skin. When I feel the circle release, I exhale slowly.

The middle of Cross's chest has a pale net of light over the blackened section of the symbol. As I watch, bits of the red energy fizzle and hiss against the blue-white light, sparking against the threads but not breaking through.

I close my eyes and fight back a smile.

When I wake up, Cross isn't in bed, and I find him humming quietly to himself in the kitchen as he goes about making a pot of coffee. He's shimmying to whatever song he's singing, little twists of his hips and legs that have me eyeing the lean bulk of him with intent. I cough quietly, and he startles, spinning around and spilling coffee grounds on the floor with a curse.

"Jesus, Kim, warn a guy," he says with a laugh as he sets the container on the counter and goes for the broom.

All of the happy warmth in my chest cools as he faces me fully. Where the binding was thick and bright the night before, it's faded now. I can see where threads have dissolved under the constant pressure of the red energy, and as I watch, another one fizzles out. Slowly, the line of power knits itself back together, but the energy is persistent and corrodes the thread.

I've bought us time, I think, but not nearly as much as I need. Not as much as Cross needs. Even though the binding is theoretically stronger than the first, it's still failing. It's not hard to figure out that it means the energy is growing in intensity, even as we try to weaken it.

"Hey, lend a hand here." Cross knocks me from my thoughts as he pushes past me with a broom. "Can you put that away while I get this swept up?"

Numbly, I take the container of grounds, put the lid on it, and tuck it into the cupboard. Cross moves around me with ease, sweeping up the grounds into a neat pile before pushing them into the dustpan. After he throws them out, he puts the broom up against the wall, then steps in close, his hands on my hips.

"How'd you sleep?" he asks, dropping a gentle kiss on my lips.

"Fine." A bit of red energy slips through the net and falls onto the floor next to my foot. I can feel the heat of it against the curl of my instep. My nerves sing.

"What about you?"

"Pretty good. I'm still feeling a bit run down this morning, though. Cup of coffee will help." He kisses me again, drawing me closer to his body. I put my hand up, and it lands in the center of his chest. I grit my teeth at the pain the touch brings with it. "What do you want to do today?"

"Let's get out of the city." The words sound far away. "I've got a place we could hole up in, get away from it all."

"You have a place," he says, teasing. "How many surprises do you have for me, Phillips?"

More than you know. I pull my hand away and step out of the circle of his arms. "I need to run to my apartment and get a few things together, and then we can hit the road. I'll be back in a few hours?"

"Sounds good. You want a coffee to go?"

"No, thanks." I'm wide awake now.

Amazing how terror can do that for you.

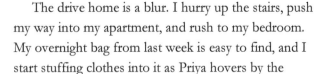

The drive home is a blur. I hurry up the stairs, push my way into my apartment, and rush to my bedroom. My overnight bag from last week is easy to find, and I start stuffing clothes into it as Priya hovers by the bedroom door.

Kim, she says hesitantly, *what do you think you're doing?*

We've got to get him out of here, I Send before grabbing a flannel shirt and discarding it. *That binding is already failing, and once it does, I don't know how we stop that tear from growing any worse. Peterson's already looking for where this extra power is coming from, and you don't have to be a genius to figure out that it's…*

I sigh. *Once the bindings fail, they're going to find him. Peterson knows what to look for. Her people know what to look for. It's only a matter of time before they put together the pieces. She's going to figure out that things started going sideways right before Emma's case was closed, and then she'll come looking for me. And for Riley.*

And you want to, what? Run away? She somehow manages to make her annoyance soft. *She's the strongest Seer in the Midwest, Kim. You can't run from her.*

I need more time. We're not going to find that here. Once I get Cross somewhere safe, Andrea and I can work on another binding, find a different way to—

Kim.

I stop, another shirt crumpled in my fist.

Priya continues, her voice soft but firm. *What are you really doing right now?*

Staring at the mess of clothes pushed into the duffel, some half-hanging out of the zippered opening, I can't answer her, though I could. I know what I'm doing. I know what running looks like, the way it feels. It's not the first time I've tried to escape a problem, and it probably won't be the last.

But there's no way to escape this one. The hole in Cross's chest is getting worse. Peterson will find us, eventually. There's no way she can't. My powers are still changing, still growing, and I have no idea what'll happen when I eventually get all the Affinities—I can't pretend anymore that that isn't where this is going. There's a kaleidoscope of color behind my eyes in Second-Sight, the mix of color now gilded with the holographic shimmer of Seeing.

I finish stuffing my clothes into the duffel and step out of the closet to meet Priya's steady gaze.

I don't know what else to do.

Why won't you tell him what's happening? You know he can't see the wound in his chest. If he could, he would've already said something. Even without knowing it's there, Riley's going to figure out that something's wrong. How do you think he'll feel when he realizes you knew the whole time and didn't say anything?

I stare into the dark interior of my closet. Light from outside glances into the darkness with me, catching the gilt edge of a book thrown haphazardly into the back corner. I don't remember Andrea giving the book back to me, but it must have been in my duffel and fallen into the closet when I put it away. Almost against my will, I bend down and pick the book up, staring at the symbol on the back cover, the same symbol decaying in the center of Cross's chest.

Stuffing the book into my duffel, I zip it shut before I can think too hard about what I'm doing.

Once I get Cross out of the city, I'll talk to him. At her glare, I roll my eyes. *I promise, Priya. I didn't mean for it to go on this long already. You're right. He needs to know what's happening.*

She nods. *Good.*

I silently hope I'm not lying to the both of us when I

say, *I promise. I'll tell him.*

It's been years since I was last at my folks' place. Honestly, I don't like thinking about it much, or, for that matter, about them. The house is hidden from the road by a tall hedge, and rows of old oak trees cover the gravel drive in shadows and acorns. It all crunches like dried bones under my tires, popping and skittering as I draw closer to the darkened hulk of the house.

Two stories and off-white with age and disrepair, it's less intimidating than I remember. The front garden beds should be choked with weeds, but all I can see are the yellow heads of daffodils trying their best to bloom between the ragged remains of last years' blossoms. It's almost relentlessly forlorn and hopeful at the same time, the dream of a white picket fence and children's laughter lost in the piles of dead leaves and the broken spindles of the wraparound porch. The windows stare out at me like dark eyes, and I startle when Cross shifts in the seat next to me, half-mumbled words tumbling from his mouth as he wakes.

"Are we there?" he asks as he runs a hand over his face. Rubbing at his eyes, he yawns wide enough for his jaw to crack. "Where the hell are we?"

"Middle of nowhere," I say and pull in front of the house. I kill the engine, and it ticks quietly as I gather the strength to let go of the steering wheel and open the door. "C'mon, let's get you inside."

Cross twists around to grab the duffel from the back

seat and winces with the motion.

Priya, I Send as he drags the bag into his lap and rubs his chest. *Anything you can do?*

She hovers near him but shakes her head. *This is more than I can handle, Kim. You're going to have to do it this time.*

I nod and slam the door. Cross clambers out of his side a moment later and waits for me to lead the way to the front door. Dropping into Second-Sight, I stare at the hole in his chest. Even with the binding still holding, it's grown again. He places his hand right over it to rub at the ache there, and his fingers barely touch the edges. When he pulls his hand back, red power drips from his fingers like blood, and I wrench my eyes away, blinking into normal sight and fighting the sick feeling in my stomach.

The lock is a bit rusty when I force the key into the knob. I twist it viciously, worried for a second that the key might break off in the lock, but with a groan, it releases. The hinges don't squeak, but the air tastes musty and old, as if it's grown unfamiliar with people breathing it.

"Nice place you got here, Phillips," Cross says as he steps past me into the front room. "Very welcoming."

The problem is that it used to be. There are white drop cloths covering the furniture, and it's dim and hard to see inside. My memories fill in the gaps, clearing away the dirt and grime, brightening the faded paint and filling the room with light. Mom used to keep flowers on the mantel, and there was a bench by the door where we'd keep our shoes in an untidy pile until she guilted us into cleaning them up, Dad leaning in close and conspiratorial as we listed places we could hide her shoes.

"You coming in?" Cross asks, shaking me from my memories.

I close the door and join him.

"Sorry about that. Let's get this place cleaned up a bit, yeah?"

It doesn't take us long to remove the drop cloths, and though the furniture is over a decade out of style, it's well made and still soft when Cross eases himself onto the couch. There's still power—I never managed to talk myself into shutting it off after I became responsible for the place when my grandmother died—and the lamp in the corner brightens the space up a bit. It doesn't fight off the sense of disuse that clings to everything, though, instead bringing it into sharper contrast.

I leave the duffel at the base of the stairs, not ready to go up and start figuring out if my nightmares will be better in my childhood bedroom or my parents'.

The whole time we tidy, I can't stop myself from rambling about the house. I fill the empty spaces in the rooms with information about the woman who checks the place for me on a monthly basis, the way it took forever for the mail to stop being sent to the house instead of the PO box my grandmother set up, the leak in the basement from two years ago that turned it into a small pond and took three days to dry out.

Cross is kind enough to not say anything about my

obvious nerves and makes quiet noises of acknowledgment that let my worry, with nothing to feed off of, fade into nothing.

"You think there's a broom around here?" he asks, eyeing the dust-covered floor.

I gesture toward the front hall closet. "In there, probably. I think I left one there the last time I was through."

He goes digging through the closet and comes up, triumphant, with a broom and dustpan. A moment later, he's sweeping his way through the living room, making tidy piles of dead ants and dust, and gathering it all together in the dustpan. I leave him to it, heart pounding as I at last find the courage to reacquaint myself with the house.

Though she doesn't have much to say, Priya stays close. I know she can sense my unease through our bond, and she Sends a burst of calm and love through it. It helps a bit, though the feelings fade quickly in the face of my memories.

I hate it here, but there's nowhere else to go, nowhere else where Cross will be as safe while I figure everything out. Not for the first time, I wish that I weren't still so pissed off at Taka, that I could lay this burden at his feet and have him carry it for me. Walking with the ghosts of my parents metaphorically haunting every corner of this house doesn't help.

We eventually settle in the front room, though there isn't much to do. I run my fingers across the spines of the books still left, and Cross settles on the couch, quiet.

"You don't talk about them," he says as he watches me. Though his voice is calm and steady, his body is tense and his eyes watchful. "Your parents, I mean."

I shrug, hoping for nonchalance instead of defensiveness. "Not much to talk about."

He gives the shabby room a meaningful look, eyebrow raised as I cross my arms. "Right. No reason to talk about you owning a house on what appears to be a massive piece of property out in the middle of nowhere that you've never mentioned before."

"They left it to me."

He stares at me, silent and waiting.

I swallow. "In their will. After they died, though my grandmother took care of it until she passed."

"Do you want to talk about it?"

"Do I look like I want to talk about it?"

Kim, Priya admonishes. *Is it so bad that he wants to know more about you?*

When it's about my parents? Yes.

He frowns at me. "I can feel you Sending."

"Then stop trying to listen in."

"I would if I could." He turns away from me, his arm coming off the back of the couch so he can rub his chest again. His hand is smeared red and black with power when he puts it on his knee. "I don't seem to have much control over it these days."

I exhale as smoothly as I can, trying not to show my unease before I join him on the couch and place my hand over top of his. The touch burns, but I keep the pain from showing. "We'll figure it out. It's going to take some time."

He laces our fingers together, palm to palm, and this time, I can't hide the wince. "Kim," he says, voice unsteady. "Have I… Look, I know what happened with Cooper—"

"Riley, that's not—"

"Just let me talk, okay?" He squeezes my hand again, stares at where our fingers touch. "I know what happened with Cooper, when I… went away, was a big deal. A *really* big deal. And I know you're doing your best to figure out what's going on so that it doesn't happen again, but if it's changed something for you, if it's changed how you feel about me, you don't have to force it. I get it. This is new, and this is… *I'm* a lot to take on right now. If you need some space or some time, I can… I'll wait, at least for a bit, while you get your head right." He looks up at me through his eyelashes, green eyes dark and sincere. "It hasn't changed anything for me."

Maybe it's the dust, maybe it's because we're in my parents' empty and abandoned living room, maybe it's because I'm fucking exhausted. Whatever the cause, my eyes ache and start to water. I can't look away from our hands, from the energy sizzling against my skin.

"That's not it."

His question is soft and low, gentle when it has every right not to be. "Then what is it?"

I follow the line of his arm to his shoulder, then to his chest, to the gaping hole in the middle of his chest, to the red seeping from it slow and steady like a broken faucet that refuses to be repaired.

"I'm scared."

His hand spasms in mine. "Of this?"

All I can manage is a quick shake of my head. "No. Not this."

"Kim." He says my name like it's exhausting, like it's too much. "You can talk to me."

"I was fourteen when they died."

The room stills. It's like everything around us pauses. Even the weak light filtering its way through the windows stops.

I keep talking.

"I was living with Taka by then, but I still saw them on the weekends. It wasn't bad, not really, not the way it had been before... It was some kind of good. And then they were driving late at night and hit some black ice, and it was kind of... awful after that."

"You loved them."

Throat tight, I nod. It's the truth, even if it's not the full shape of it. And though it hurts, it's easier to talk about my dead parents than it is to try explaining to Cross that he's got a portal to Death breaking open in his chest.

"I'm sorry you lost them," he continues, his hand gentle on mine. "I don't know what I'd do without my family."

I fight the urge to laugh. I lost my parents long before they died, lost them as soon as I started talking

to ghosts and brushing up against Death. They knew
something was wrong before I did. All I saw were their
wary glances, their carefully constructed distances. I hid
what I could and laughed off what I couldn't, and it
worked for a while. It worked until the ghosts started
gathering and Turning, until my grandmother saw and
knew.

Everything my grandmother did for me was good,
but snatching me from this house was the best thing she
could have done. She protected me. Kept me safe. Her
daughter should have known better, but Mom…

It doesn't matter now. They're both dead, and
Grandma Sadie is dead, and Cross is dying. He's
bleeding out and doesn't know it, and I can't stanch the
flow.

"Hey." His hand on my cheek is so gentle, I feel like
shattering against it. "Hey, Kim, it's okay. C'mere."

He draws me into his arms, and though it burns, I
fall against his body easily. I bury my face in his
shoulder, my hands on his chest where the wound
doesn't touch, and I let him whisper nonsense into my
hair and run his broad hands over my back.

I love him.

We'll figure it out, Priya Sends. The words are like fire
in my mind, filled with determination and more than a
hint of fear. *We have to.*

She doesn't say anything else and simply places her
cool, indistinct hand over Cross's, and, for a moment, I
let them take the weight from my shoulders.

But only for a moment.

I end up putting our bags in my old room. The bed, a queen I'd wheedled and begged my parents into getting me, is still in decent shape. It sags a bit in the middle, and the drop cloth on the top didn't keep all the dust from the bedding, but it'll do for now. There's a washer and dryer in the basement, and if we're lucky enough, there might be some laundry detergent still down there, too. I'm too tired to consider washing anything right now, though, and once I wrestle my boots off, I fall face-first onto the bed.

"Graceful," Cross says from somewhere else in the room. The door closes with a soft click and only a bit of squealing hinges. I listen to him moving about the room, relaxing into sharing a space with someone. A moment later, the bed dips, and I roll slightly to the side.

Cross smiles down at me, soft and fond.

"You think the water heater's any decent?" he asks, oblivious to my suddenly racing heart.

I shrug, aiming for nonchalance and likely missing. "Probably."

"Great." Digging through the duffel, he comes up with a pair of sweatpants. "I'm going to take a quick shower."

"There should be towels in the hall closet, though no promises on how clean they are."

"Great," he says with a forced smile. "I'll be right back."

Once he steps out of the room, I throw my legs over the edge of the bed, rest my arms on my thighs, and put my head in my hands. Burying my fingers in my hair, I count breaths for a handful of moments, trying to swallow down my fear and grief.

I'm so scared of what's happening to Cross, what it means that we can't stem the tide. It doesn't matter what Andrea and I throw at it. Whatever is happening in the center of Cross's chest isn't stopping—it's moving inexorably forward. I think back to that parking lot, those black and red eyes gleaming from Cross's face, and fight back nausea.

If it is Baker, I won't let him take Riley again. I've nearly lost him twice now, and I refuse to consider it happening a third time.

Being here, in my childhood home, isn't helping my emotional state, either. The place has its share of happy memories, sure, but a lot of them are far from picturesque.

When I first started showing signs of the Sight, my mom didn't handle it well. You would think with her mom being a Burner that she would have known what to expect, would have had some sense of what it meant when her daughter started talking to people who weren't there. But no. Mom didn't even have a hint of the Sight, and all she saw of her mother was this larger-than-life character who talked to creatures that Mom could never see. When her daughter started doing the same thing, instead of recognizing it for what it was, she put it down to imaginary friends and an overly creative child. It didn't matter that those imaginary friends had broken arms and blood trickling from their mouths. She simply yelled at my dad for letting me watch his action flicks, made him save them for after I went to bed, and that was the end of it.

I knew it made her uncomfortable. Kids aren't stupid, and I knew that talking to my ghosts made Mom unhappy. So I stopped talking to them out loud. They heard me when I thought things at them. I didn't need to speak to be heard.

Over time, though, they started to Turn, though I didn't know what was happening at the time. They teach kids about it in schools, but I was never a good student, never paid enough attention to my teachers when I should have, and somehow, that lesson missed me when I dearly needed it not to. So when my friends' eyes turned black, and their brief flashes of anger grew longer, more intense, I did my best to protect myself against them but never thought to ask for help. Some nascent instinct in my blood told me to keep silver nearby, to put chalk along the edges of my room at night, but it was only a matter of time before someone got hurt.

Thankfully, Grandma Sadie visited before that happened.

God, she was so mad. First at me for talking to ghosts when I should know better, when she'd tried to teach me what school hadn't been able to. Then at my mom for not calling her sooner, for being ashamed of her daughter and her skills. I was twelve, well past when most kids developed the Sight, and Mom never told Grandma Sadie that she had concerns, that she thought I might have the Sight.

That Burning was quick and brutal. No careful scribing of circles, no talking to the ghosts to try convincing them to cross on their own without a fight. No, Sadie had wrapped power around her like a shroud, grabbed those half-Turned ghosts by their throats, and dragged them into Death before they even knew what was happening.

It was the first time I remember being afraid of her, and her—our—power.

Grandma took me with her that night, my mom sobbing on the front porch but not stopping us. Sadie's grip on my wrist had been rough, her fingers digging into the thin skin and bones. Part of me wanted to struggle, wanted to pull away and stay with my parents and the illusion of safety they offered. But the other part of me, the stronger part, knew that Grandma Sadie would never hurt me, that I could trust her, that she saw the things I did, talked to the things I did. She could help me learn to be brave.

Now, decades later, I'm sick with fear.

It doesn't matter that I'm more powerful than I've ever been in my life. It doesn't matter that I have an expert in scribing on my side, that I've got years and years of experience dealing with the Turned, that I have been through the crucible and back. All of the skills and competency I've depended on my entire life are worthless in the face of Cross's decaying body and

Death pushing its way back through the collapsing barrier between it and Life. One way or another, something is going to break through, and nausea makes me gag at the thought of the destruction that might bring if it succeeds.

Angry and frustrated, I undress. By the time Cross comes back from his shower, I'm curled on the far side of the bed, knees tucked into my chest, eyes closed as I feign sleep. He quietly gets ready for bed, and I let the sound of him moving around the room soothe me. The mattress dips when he climbs into it, and as he shuffles closer, wrapping me in his arms, I breathe through the pain of his wound and its caustic energy pressed up against my back.

It's a long time before I fall asleep, my body aching the whole way down.

CHAPTER THIRTEEN

My sleep is fitful and filled with massive bodies roaming across a gray plain. They don't turn to look at me, but I see their eyes shift to me whirling in the sunken sockets of their skulls. Arms swinging, their lumbering steps shaking the ground beneath me, I stand still and watch them move in the hazy distance, knowing they're watching me watching them.

I wake up well before dawn. Cross rolled onto his other side at some point in the middle of the night, and he's curled in on himself on the other side of the bed. Sweat beads on his forehead, and his skin's lost the rosy glow it had the day before. Instead, it's turned a pallid gray, and I pull the blanket up closer around his neck, tucking him in before I go.

Padding my way downstairs and into the kitchen, I start a pot of coffee. There's no coffee maker, only an old-style percolator, and I fill it with water. We picked up groceries the night before, and I take out the coffee from the almost-bare pantry. Once I scoop out the grounds, I light the burner and set the percolator on top. After, as I go to clean up, I hold the bag of grounds in my hands for a long moment and set it down on the counter carefully, waiting for the percolator to finish.

You're going to have to talk to him.

I groan before pressing my head into my hands. *It's too early for this conversation.*

You can't keep ignoring it.

I know that, Priya. You've convinced me it's a good fucking idea to talk to Cross about the goddamned portal into Death forming in the middle of his fucking chest. Jesus.

You got yourself into this mess, Kim. Don't snap at me because it's finally time to clean it up.

I know. I push the hair from my face and tilt my head back. *Just… If it is Baker behind the power, and he's trying to escape Death, then he's not going to stop, not when there's an obvious weakness between Life and Death that keeps getting weaker. And we don't know… It's already hurting Riley, and Baker isn't even through yet.*

Priya settles next to me, her face a mask of somber strength. *We won't know what's going to happen to Riley until it happens. But he needs to know before then. He knows something is wrong, Kim.*

How do I tell him, though?

With patience and understanding. He's going to be mad.

He's going to be furious.

She sighs. *Probably. Doesn't mean it shouldn't be done.*

She's right, though I hate to admit it, even to myself. I've waited too long to tell him what's happening, and now, I have to deal with the repercussions of my fear.

I get comfortable on the living room couch and

drink my coffee slowly while I wait for sunrise. Priya doesn't bother manifesting, choosing to give me space. I appreciate it, but I also feel more alone than I have in years.

Sitting by myself, in the silence of my dead parents' home, I'm forced to acknowledge the worst-case scenarios. Binding Cross the same way Baker was would cut him off from Death. If he hadn't spent the last six months learning how to be a Medium, if he hadn't been swimming in Death's power—even unknowingly—for the same amount of time, I wouldn't hesitate to do it. It's the cleanest cut, the most surgical option.

But Cross has changed because of his contact with that power, and cutting him off cold turkey? I have no idea what'll happen, but it's unlikely to be anything good. He's already weak. How would his body—his soul—respond to having that extra power stripped away?

The smaller bindings are holding things at bay, but I can't spend the rest of my life casting those over and over again. I doubt Baker would stop, even if I did. His single-minded determination to come back into Life is the whole reason this entire debacle started. There's no way he'll give up after being barely stopped a handful of times.

I can't put it off any longer.

I drink my coffee, and I wait.

I must fall asleep at some point, because when I

wake up again, the sun is glinting through the windows, and Cross is sitting by my feet on the couch, his hand resting on my ankle as his thumb slides over the bone.

"Hey," he says with a squeeze, "you okay?"

"Yeah." I rub my eyes and sit up, pulling my foot away. I miss his touch as soon as it's gone. "Just couldn't sleep. I didn't want to bother you."

"You're no bother. Pass me your mug."

I hand him the coffee cup, and he gets up and heads to the kitchen. There's the quiet noise of coffee being poured into porcelain, and he comes back with two steaming mugs. As he settles back on the couch, he hands one to me and waits until I take a careful sip.

"It's good," I say, staring in the dark liquid instead of his eyes.

"So." I feel him shift, the cushions dipping as he gets more comfortable on the couch. "Are you finally going to tell me what's going on?"

I snap my head up. Coffee sloshes over the rim of the mug and scalds my fingers, but the sting is less distracting than my surprise.

He almost looks disappointed. "Did you really think I didn't know you were keeping something from me? Kim. I'm a detective."

"I…"

His voice is hard when he says, "You can either keep lying to me, or you can tell me the truth."

Setting my coffee down on the table, I pull my legs close to my body and settle my arms around them. I feel small and childish, but it's a tiny bit of comfort.

I should be stronger than this.

"I don't really know where to start."

"Try from the beginning," he says, fingers brushing the top of my foot for a brief moment before pulling away, "and we'll figure out the rest."

The words spill out of me haltingly at first, but with greater speed as the dam breaks. I talk about Baker and Death, the power flooding the city, its impact on ghosts and people.

On us.

"It's why you're a Medium, why I have these new Affinities, why Priya is…"

"Wait, what's happening with Priya?"

She's sitting in the corner of the room, watching us silently. With a sigh, she floats closer, then holds her hand out toward Cross. As it nears his chest, the skin starts to darken, then crack.

"What is…" His eyes are wide when they meet mine. "I'm doing that to her?"

"Yes and no." I watch as she pulls away and her skin smooths back out. "The energy makes ghosts Turn."

He continues to stare at Priya until she fades away. Sadness pulses through our bond, and my heart aches.

"I thought bonded ghosts couldn't."

"I'm not entirely sure about that, but I'm not sure about a lot of things anymore."

Cross doesn't say anything else and sits in the oppressive silence. My coffee is cold, but I drink some anyway, my hands needing something to do.

"Were you ever going to tell me?" he asks at last.

I nod but can't meet his eyes.

"How long were you going to wait?"

"I was waiting for you to wake up."

He huffs out a breath. "Right."

"I mean it." My voice shakes, but my words are heavy, solid. "I should have told you sooner, but I *was* going to talk to you this morning."

"We've talked about this before, Kim. I don't like it when you keep secrets from me." His frown deepens. "I definitely don't like it when my life is in the balance."

My eyes stare back at me from the uneven surface of the coffee.

"But I haven't exactly been honest with you, either."

I look up and find that he's staring at his hands, which are clasped together in his lap, his knuckles white.

"If we're telling each other the truth, then..."

His smile is a dim, wasted version of its usual self. "Yeah. Well... I've been hearing voices. Not all the time, but they're there. Almost like background noise or... or a radio that isn't tuned fully to a station. It started up about four weeks ago, before everything that happened with Cooper." He looks at Priya, the furrow between his brows deepening. "And Second-Sight's gotten weird, too. I'm seeing in it all the time now, even when I'm not trying to. But it's... Well, it's *different*."

"Different how?"

"What's the room look like to you?" he asks,

meeting my eyes.

I drop fully into Second-Sight and take in the space. Energy outlines everything in a shifting kaleidoscope of color. Priya waits nearby, her eyes gray and her hair floating sedately around her face. Other than the three of us, though, there's nothing of interest in the room or the spaces in between.

"Like a room."

"Yeah…" His voice sours. "Not to me. There's…" He trails off, eyes darting to the corners. "People, I guess."

"How many?"

"Five now. There was another earlier, but they left. I don't know where they went."

I look carefully around the room again and shiver. Whatever Cross is seeing, it's not visible in Second-Sight. "Voices no one else can hear and ghosts no one else can see. How long have you been seeing them?"

"Since the building collapse, after Cooper ran."

"Well." I take another tepid sip. "At least we know when things changed. What do you remember from… when it happened?"

"Not much. A lot of pain, at least at first. And then… I was outside of myself, but my body was moving. There was this… *thing* clinging to my chest, and I had to tear it off before I was back."

"Right before you passed out," I whisper, "your eyes were black. And red."

None of us speak for a long time.

It's Baker, Priya says after a while. *He broke through and took over your body to Burn that ghost.*

Cross nods. "That's what I was thinking, too."

"He's trying to do it again." My hands shake. "It's why your chest hurts, why that power's coming through. But I don't understand *why* he's trying to do it. He wanted to go from Life into Death before. Why's he trying to go the other way now?"

We're missing something.

"Yeah, no shit." I wince. "Sorry. I just... I want to stop it, stop him."

"It should be easier now that I know what's going on." Cross's words cut. "I'll be able to let you know how I'm feeling, what symptoms I'm having. I won't think I'm losing my mind."

"I'm sorry, okay?" I get up from the couch, then wonder where the hell I should go now that I'm standing. "I'll... Fuck, I'll just go."

I head toward the stairs, but I stop when he calls my name.

"Where are you going to go?" He stands and gestures around the room, to the vast expanse of farmland around us. "Running away is only going to make this worse."

"But you want me to go," I say. "You don't want me here."

"Kim." He takes a hesitant step toward me, then stops. "Look, you fucked up. You lied to me. But... I get it, okay? I was lying, too. We're both at fault here, but even if we weren't, that doesn't mean I want you to fuck off forever, okay? But I'm allowed to be pissed about it, same as you're allowed to be pissed at me."

"But I'm not."

"Well, that's your prerogative. I'd be pretty mad if I were in your shoes."

It's my fault, is what I want to say. *You wouldn't be hearing voices or seeing the dead if it weren't for me.*

What I say instead is, "We should make sure the binding is holding."

His hand rests on his chest, and he winces at the touch. Nodding, he reaches for the hem of his shirt. When he pulls it over his head and away, I gasp.

The woven net of power is frayed and failing in multiple spots. There are entire sections that are hanging on by sheer willpower, and even those tendrils of power appear to be giving way as I watch. The red-black energy spilling from his chest pulses, and it swells and pours out of his chest to land in a heavy, spectral blob between his feet. It flows sluggishly toward me, and my powers lash out at it, cutting into the power like a sparking whip. Where my power hits, the red-black energy curls back like the burned edges of a page. But there's so much of it, it oozes over the charred edges and creeps closer.

Shivering, I step to the side and let it sluggishly move past. Priya watches from the other side of the room, her eyes thankfully gray but serious and sad.

"It's still holding," I say, though my voice cracks. "But it's going to fail. Probably soon."

He rubs his chest. "How long do you think we have?"

"Not long enough." I swallow down my growing panic. "But I think I can find a way to buy us time."

He frowns. "Another binding?"

"No, I don't think the bindings are doing anything but slowing it. We need to contain it fully, control it."

"We don't know how to do that, though."

"But we know someone who does."

CHAPTER FOURTEEN

P eterson's office hasn't changed much since the last time I visited. It's unsettling how similar it is to when I was last here, telling her about Emma. I wonder if Peterson will hold any fondness for me because of that, or if everything that's happened since then will have rubbed her goodwill out like a stain.

"Detective." Peterson rises from behind her desk, her gray hair neatly pinned to the top of her head. She's wearing a dark blue pantsuit, her white shirt underneath crisp and neatly creased. A gold necklace hangs in the hollow of her throat, and she pinches the pendant between her fingers, dragging it back and forth along the chain. The metal glints in the fluorescent lights of her office as she walks toward me.

"I have to admit, I didn't expect to see you again so soon." Her smile is sharp.

"Well, you know what they say. Things always happen when you least expect them."

"Considering how often I expect things, it's still a bit of a surprise." She gestures to a small seating area, but I stay standing. "Of course. Shall we get right into it, then?"

Turning her back to me, she wanders to the floor-to-ceiling windows overlooking the lake. The sun's setting and casting long shadows across the water like fingers reaching for the horizon. Her silhouette is simply another dark smear across the bloodred water.

"Since the last time we spoke, I've Seen a few things, including where that power is coming from." Her smile softens, but only a little. "I understand why you wouldn't want to tell me. He's very important to you, isn't he?"

I stiffen. "What do you want?"

As she glances over her shoulder to look at me, the barest edge of a smile crosses her lips. "The same thing I wanted when we last spoke. The tears must be sealed. The energy flow must be contained. There's only one way to guarantee it."

"I won't let you hurt him."

She laughs. "My dear, it is admirable that you would want to protect your… partner, but do you honestly think you could keep him safe if I wanted him hurt? You forget who I am."

"I know exactly who you are," I snap. "You're yet another person who thinks the only solution to a problem is to destroy it."

"Do you understand what we're facing here, Detective?" She gestures to the lake, the wave of her arm somehow encapsulating the entirety of the city, even though the only visible part of it is the thin sliver along the lakefront. "Everyone you've ever known, everyone you've ever loved, all of their lives are at risk right now because of what is happening to your partner. If enough of that energy crosses into Life, they will all die because you refuse to sacrifice one man. It's a romantic idea, though misguided."

I stare out over the water, fighting for breath.

What do you want to do? Priya asks, her voice unsteady. *What are you going to do?*

"There has to be another way. You've contained it with the markers before, there's got to be something you can do to help him, to stop it."

Peterson's expression softens again. "I promise you, there isn't. The markers are failing, and I've tried to See every future, but all I find is destruction. A vast, gray emptiness. The dead walking with what little remains of the living. There are no cities, no forests, no mountains. Only… nothingness. Unless you—"

"I *can't.*"

"You would be amazed what you can do when pressed to it." She lets the necklace drop from between her fingers and stuffs her hand into her pocket. "I know he's not in the city. You can speed this along by telling us where he is or, better yet, bringing him to us. I promise you, we only want what's best."

"Best for you."

Her voice shakes as she shouts, "Best for everyone!" She stalks toward me, her eyes dark with anger. "I have been more than patient with you. I have given you time to say goodbye, which is more than I've been afforded in the past. It is time to *let him go*, Detective, or I will be forced to take him from you instead."

I laugh. "I'd like to see you try."

She stills, her expression falling into a carefully managed mask of neutrality. "Of course." Lifting a hand, she waves toward the corner of the room. "Security, if you'd be so kind."

A hidden door opens, and two heavily muscled men in suits—one tall and whipcord lean with light hair, the other brawnier and with a heavy, black beard—step out of it. They've got guns on their hips, and their hands hover over their holsters.

I look at Peterson, anger building in my gut. "You don't want to do this."

"You've given me no choice." She steps back, making way for the guards. "Now, you can come quietly—"

The laugh punches out of me before I can stop it, and the guards take it as their signal to approach. I fall into a fighting stance, my weight on my back foot.

"I'm a fucking detective," I bite out as they draw closer, one shifting to the side to try to flank me. "You think I haven't been in a fight before?"

"We don't want to hurt you, ma'am," the blond says, holding his hands up placatingly, but I can see the subtle tense of his muscle the second before he darts forward, reaching for my wrists.

I shift my weight to my back foot, and he misses. Off-balance, it's a simple matter to step to his side and get my foot under his ankle. He trips forward, stumbling for a brief moment before regaining his balance. Meanwhile, the bearded one rushes forward, and his shoulder crashes into mine, pushing me into one of the chairs. I catch myself before I tumble over it, but when I come up, he's got his hand around my wrist, grip tight and unyielding.

"You don't want to do that," I say as I pull power into my body.

He yanks me toward him, his other hand already reaching for my free arm, and I *push*. Orange light bursts from my body and smacks him in the chest. His feet lift from the floor as he's thrown back, his mouth open in a breathless gasp. It wrenches my wrist, but he doesn't hold on, too surprised from being flung across the room to keep his grip.

"I warned you," I say as I take a step toward the elevator door.

Peterson's eyes are wide as she stares at me. "That doesn't... You're a Burner."

I hurry to the elevator and slap the down button while the bearded guard slowly gets to his feet. "Yeah, about that..."

Looking to the blond one for a quick moment, the bearded guard gives a sharp nod, and the pair of them charge me. My back's at the elevator door, and with nowhere to run, I grab power, throw it in a wide loop across the floor, and pull as soon as their feet pass through the orange light. They fall onto the floor with a sickening smack, and I grab more power before wrapping it around their wrists. Turning them both onto their backs with a wave of light, I grapple for their ankles. It's more than I can control, though, and the blond one shakes free of my psychic grip.

The elevator dings behind me.

"You can't be a Shaker," Peterson says quietly. "It doesn't work that way."

"Something I've learned over the last year?" I step back into the open elevator and hit the ground floor button. The elevator chimes cheerfully, and as the doors shut, I say, "Things tend to not work around me."

What a zinger, Priya says, deadpan. *She'll be feeling that for weeks.*

Shut up. I rub at my wrist, which is starting to ache from where the guard grabbed me. *What do you think our chances are that the lobby won't be filled with guards?*

Pretty slim. She floats closer to me, then reaches with her power to Heal the ache in my arm. *They're probably already there.*

We could get out on another floor, take a fire exit?

She nods. *Probably a good idea.*

I rest against the wall, tipping my head back until it thumps against the metal. *I think that's the first good idea I've had since this started.*

Oh, they haven't all been awful.

I laugh. *Tell me one thing I've done that hasn't bit us in the ass.*

You started going for coffee at that one place near HQ, the one with the good danishes.

Ha ha, very funny. You know that's not what I meant.

I know.

Silence falls like a lead weight. The elevator hums,

and I lean forward to hit whatever buttons I can reach. Half the panel lights up, and a moment later, the car comes to a halt on the sixteenth floor.

Wait for another one? I ask, looking at the lower floors still lit up on the panel.

Better to send them an empty car and buy us more time to get out of here.

I sigh, then stop the door from shutting. Before leaving, I press all of the remaining floors and hope it's enough to buy us time.

Thankfully, the fire exit is clearly marked, and with a bit of careful Shaking, the alarmed door doesn't trigger. By the time we reach the ground floor, my legs are screaming and I'm cursing every day I skipped my cardio.

I hate this, I say as we spill out into a dim alleyway.

Exercise?

No, sneaking around like criminals. We're better than this.

Not currently, we're not. Priya peeks around the edge of the building, then nods. *Coast's clear. They're watching the lobby, not the street.*

Great. As casually as possible, I walk out of the alley and toward the corner. The car is parked a few blocks away, more than enough space between us and Peterson's building to avoid detection, but waiting on the corner for the light makes me feel like I've got a target on my back.

The light changes, and I step off the curb, feeling like there's absolutely nothing wrong.

As soon as we're no longer in sight of Peterson's building, the tension drains from my body. *That was stupid. I don't know why I thought she'd be able to help.*

It was a good idea, Priya says. *You didn't know how it was going to go.*

I shake my head. *No, I didn't, but I could guess. The markers are failing. We've known that this whole time. Even if she had been willing to help us, her bindings probably would've failed, like ours. On top of that, she doesn't know Cross. She doesn't care about him. Why would she hesitate to do what needs to be done?*

Priya stops, eyes wide. I keep walking.

What do you mean what needs *to be done?*

Baker has to be stopped. That energy has to be stopped.

Yeah, but what you're saying…

I know. I want to throw something, but there's nothing in my pockets that I'm willing to part with. Instead, I kick at a piece of loose sidewalk and watch as it skitters over the concrete and into the street. *I'm out of ideas here.*

I want things fixed as much as you do, Priya says. *Maybe even more so. But you aren't seriously considering hurting Riley.*

No, of course not. The car pops into view, and I fish my keys from my pocket. *I'm not going to hurt him. But I can't think of how to help. We've tried everything we could think of, and none of it's worked.*

There's got to be something else.

I jam my key into the lock and wrench the door open. *Like what?*

That energy hurts you, right? Priya settles in the passenger seat as I slam my door shut. *And you can Burn it away, at least a little. You've done it before.*

Buckle done, car started, I check my mirror before pulling onto the street. *It wasn't that much.*

Maybe it's enough to stave off the tide, buy us more time.

And in the meantime, all of us are exposed to more and more of that energy. I look at her, then back to the road, throat tight. *Speaking of... How're you feeling?*

Fine, more or less. It comes and goes.

What... I swallow. *What does it feel like?*

She's quiet for a long time. We come to a stop at a red light. The color leaks through the windshield and stains the interior like blood.

It's odd, but I don't feel it when it starts happening. I just... slip, I guess. The things I'm feeling, they're things I've felt for a long time. Love for you, a desire to help others, to protect. They're familiar. But then something twists, and...

And then they're not.

No, even that's not right. They are familiar. I've been angry before and possessive. But the things that stopped me from lashing out before, they're gone. The voice in my mind that told me to stop, that told me what I was doing was wrong, it's gotten quieter.

But it's still there?

She looks at me, then away. *For now.*

It's dark by the time I pull up the gravel drive of my parents' place. The windows of the house are bright, though, and as I park the car, I see Cross moving around inside. He steps out onto the porch as I climb out of the car, and though I feel stupid immediately after doing it, I give him a small wave.

"Welcome home," he says with a half smile. He holds a beer up. "You thirsty?"

I hurry up the steps and take the bottle when he offers it to me. The glass is wet with condensation, and it slips a little in my grip when he lets it go. "Very. How're you feeling?"

"I've been better, but I've been worse." He rubs his chest, and I wince as another piece of the binding falls away. "How'd your chat with Peterson go?"

"Not well." I take a sip and let myself enjoy the smooth slide of cold beer before continuing. "She's not your biggest fan."

"Shocking." He brushes past me as he walks down the steps and pauses at the bottom. "You coming?"

"Where are we going?"

He tips his chin up toward the clear night sky. "Figured I'd get some stargazing in while I still can. You can't see everything out here, but it's better than downtown."

I trail after him as he wanders into the field in front of the house. Crickets strike up a chorus as we wade through the high grass, but their noise fades as I grow used to the sound. Cross tilts his head back, lets out a sigh, and eases himself to the ground. Spreading his arms and legs out on the grass, he smooths out a space like a snow angel, and I can't help but laugh. He grins up at me, then rolls onto his side to smash down a bit more grass before patting it invitingly.

"C'mon, Phillips. Make yourself comfortable."

I pass him the beer bottle as I sit, and he takes a long drink before setting it to the side. I squeeze in next to him, resting my head in the crook of his shoulder, and his arm wraps around me to pull me closer.

The sky above us is an inky blue and dotted with stars. I never learned any of the constellations as a kid, but I connect the dots now, making up designs and figures in the sky as Cross and I pass the beer between us, neither of us speaking while the crickets chirp around us.

"I like this," he says quietly.

"Me, too." I offer him the nearly empty bottle, but he waves it away. Finishing the final mouthful, I hold the neck of the bottle between my fingers, turning it this way and that to catch the reflected light from the house in the brown glass. I wrap my fist around the neck and throw it as hard as I can into the distance. After a moment, I hear the glass shatter.

Cross's voice rumbles through my ear. "What was that for?"

"I just needed to do something." I lay back down, then wince. Red energy seeps down the side of his chest and pools on the ground. Sighing, I shift away, still sitting.

"What's left to do?" he asks, eyes solemn.

"Wait, I guess." I reach out and push against the

power, watching it fizzle away for a moment before it oozes closer. "For the binding to break or for Baker to do whatever it is he plans to do."

"Or for me to—"

"Don't." I wish I had that bottle to throw again. "Don't say it."

"We both know I'm not getting any better, Kim. Do you know what I did while you were gone? I slept. All day. I think I ate once. And this"—his hand goes to his chest, settling over the wound like a poorly placed bandage—"this feels like a hot knife, all the time. Just twisting deeper and deeper."

I fight to find the right words, to say something to smooth away the crease between his brows, but all I can come up with is a deep, steady helplessness.

I don't know what to do.

Cross winces. "Shit, something's…" He groans and rolls onto his side, his hand clenching into a fist against his chest.

The binding flares beneath his hand, blue-white light suddenly bright in the dark. One by one, the remaining threads start snapping.

Priya! I fumble for my knife. *It's failing!*

To Cross, I say, "Hold on, okay? I'll take care of it, I promise."

As the final piece of energy holding the wound together snaps, his eyes fly open. The green is gone, replaced by an empty night sky. Only now the color's bled from his irises into his sclera, and he stares at me with black eyes.

"Kim." He gasps, his hands suddenly pushing me away. "Kim, you have to run. You have to—"

And then there's an explosion, and I'm thrown like an empty beer bottle, tumbling through the air.

CHAPTER FIFTEEN

I slam into the ground and roll, my ribs aching. As I land on my hands and knees and push myself upright, I flinch. There's a great noise, like wind rushing through a canyon, like a tsunami bearing down on the shore, like all the lights in the city going off at once. It rings in my ears to the point of pain, and I clamp my hands over them, trying to stave off the sound. No matter how hard I press my hands to my head, though, the noise grows and grows, until I'm screaming and hunched over, trying to get away from it.

My voice echoes in the sudden silence, the scream ricocheting across the open field. Panting, I look up and freeze.

About twenty feet away, Cross is standing, the grass blown down around him, a circle of broken stems all pointed away from him as if they're running. He's looking at his hands, turning them over again and again, and the smile on his face isn't one I recognize. His black eyes glint as he looks at me.

"Baker," I gasp, and as I say his name, he looks up, eyes bloodred and shining.

His smile is all teeth. "Kim. It's so good to see you

again."

I struggle to my feet. There's blood running down the side of my head and sticking to my neck, wet and viscous. "Get out of him."

"Oh, I wish I could, but you know how these things are." He shrugs. "One way only, I'm afraid."

"No."

"Kim." He sounds disappointed. "You knew that this was how things were going to end. Your young man made a valiant effort to keep me out, I'll give him that, but you don't know the power that's available in Death or how much of it I've absorbed since you so rudely sent me along. As for what you did then"—he takes a step forward, the grass crackling beneath his feet—"you and I will be having a nice long chat about that."

I reach into the earth and wrench it sideways, orange light arcing with the ground as it dances beneath his feet. For a moment, he stumbles, but then he smiles, reaches forward, and grabs the lines of power. They snap and flail in his grip, but as he tightens his fist, they flare and disappear. When I go to Shake the ground again, there's a quiet roll, then nothing.

"What did you do?"

"You're a child, playing with things you don't understand. Untrained, untried, hope your only teacher." He takes another confident step forward, and though I hold my ground, I want to run. "You should know better than to hope, Kim."

His hand fills with light, and a searing ball crashes into my chest and knocks me from my feet. The air rushes from my lungs in a painful gasp, and as I stare up at the star-studded night sky, I try to remember how to breathe.

Don't you touch her, Priya snarls. Her hair is a riotous mass around her face, and her eyes are black. The color runs down her face like tears, and her skin is flayed and burned along her arms and neck. Hovering over me, red energy leaks from the fissures in her skin and drips down onto my body, stinging me with each touch.

Priya, pull it back, I Send desperately. When she turns her dark eyes to me, they swirl white for a moment before the light winks out, covered by black. *Priya, no!*

She snarls, then charges Baker. Energy crackles in the air and taints it with ozone. When Priya crashes into Baker, there's a quiet explosion. It's a force, rather than a sound, and the grass presses itself flatter against the ground as it rolls over all of us. I'm pushed away, my body dragging painfully across dirt and stones, and as I land half on my side, half on my front, I finally manage to suck in a breath. Green energy wraps itself around me, healing the cuts and scrapes covering my body and easing some of the ache in my chest. I pull it back as my survival instinct screams at me to conserve my power for whatever is coming next.

As I struggle to my feet, Priya whips around Baker like a force of nature. Power lashes between them in great streaks of lightning and sickly green tendrils of energy that wrap around Baker's arms and chest like clinging vines. Where they touch, his skin boils and bleeds. As soon as the tendrils dissipate, red energy pours forth from his wounds, mixing with blood until all I see is vile red.

His injuries heal.

He's still smiling.

Priya! I reach for our bond, praying that I can bring her back to herself. *You have to stop! He's… It's Cross. It's Riley.*

Her black eyes whirl back to me, full of puzzled innocence. *Riley?*

Yes! You have to stop. You're hurting him.

She looks at Baker again. He takes a step closer to me, light gathering in his palm again.

He wants to hurt you. Her hair whips about her face. Black bleeds down her cheeks. *No one hurts you, Kim. You're mine.*

There's that echo of ownership, that twisted memory of the love between us. It hurts as much as watching Baker pilot Cross's body does.

I'm helpless to do anything for either of them.

Please. I nearly sob the word. *You have to stop.*

Light smashes into my chest again, and I'm thrown back. I somehow remain on my feet this time. My shirt is burned, pieces of singed cotton falling to the ground in glowing red embers. They lick at the grass, and as it catches, I make out a crack of red energy hidden between the blades. It blends with the flames, both of them stinging and hot against my skin.

The energy is everywhere. I drop fully into Second-Sight and nearly gag. It writhes and twists through the earth. Veins and arteries of sickly power grow and brighten as they draw closer to Baker.

In the sharp, multicolored light of Second-Sight, he's an emaciated corpse. His skin presses into the hollows of his cheeks, into the cavernous orbits of his eye sockets. His eyes are two bright embers hidden in that darkness, his smile a rictus of teeth and gristle. He shuffles forward, legs and arms twisted as he moves when everything in my gut says he shouldn't be able to move at all. His chest is broken open, ribs peeled back to reveal the dried flesh within.

There's a spinning orb of black and red where his heart should be. It pulses slowly, the light brightening and dimming with a slow, steady tempo. The earth around me flares in time with it. Power arcs and grows from the ground to his body.

Around me, I can feel the barrier between Life and Death collapsing. It's like those pools of energy gathered around the markers, the thick ropes of red power lancing through Chicago, all of it gathered and tumbling together. There are fissures everywhere around me, thin tears, all coalescing into deeper rifts that grow with each breath Baker takes. Red bleeds through, dripping onto the ground to mix with the flames, the whole world lit by fire.

"It's too late," Baker says gleefully. "You're too late."

Priya screams. Her power lashes out, green whips that snag and tear at Baker. Growling, he turns his attention from me to her and with an almost careless gesture, he blasts pure power from his hand into her chest. It wraps around her in tangled bands of white, crushing her burned arms against her sides, covering her screaming mouth, her black, bleeding eyes. When she falls to the ground—a motion that makes no sense to my terrified mind, since Priya isn't alive, isn't held down by something as mortal as gravity—she struggles for a moment, then goes still. Her form dims, then fades.

Her voice is a whispered breath in my mind. *Kim.*

I desperately reach for her, but before I can pull her close, the echo of her voice is gone.

"What'd you do to her?" I take an uncertain step forward. "What'd you do, you bastard?"

"Nothing worse than what was happening to her already," he says.

Light gathers in his hands again, and part of me wonders if there's any point in trying to dodge it or shield against it. The flames lick at my feet and I stumble forward. One way or another, I figure I'm fucked.

Cross's face is lit from below, the sharp planes of his jaw and cheeks cast in a stark white and burning red that turns him from beloved to terrifying. I don't recognize any part of him now.

Baker continues, "I am sorry if that makes any difference. She still cared for you, as much as a Turned ghost could. And this one…" Baker looks at his body and sighs. "He was convinced it was love."

"You can't have him." I sob. Smoke burns my eyes. "He's not yours."

"Oh, dear child." Baker spins the power in his hands, sets it whirling into a vortex of white and red. "It doesn't matter who he belongs to, not anymore. He's *gone*. This body is all that remains."

I grit my teeth and reach deep. Crackling blue-white energy fills me like a wildfire springing to life.

"No."

The binding rips from me with a scream, my hands stretched forward to guide the blanket of energy toward Baker. It slams into him like a wave, the light crashing over and wrapping around him. His arms are pinned to his sides, and the ball of power in his hand falls to the ground and whirls for a brief moment before guttering out. Blue light covers him as red flames dance around me, and I feel sharp satisfaction when he struggles against the binding and it holds.

His expression is contemplative as he looks at the energy wrapped tightly around him. "I do appreciate your persistence. It's an admirable, if stupid, trait."

Flexing, he strains against the binding again. I can feel it in my gut, that flex of muscle and bone. My body aches with it. A deep-seated pain lances through me, and I cry out. Stumbling forward, I push more power into the binding. It crackles through me, stinging and awful, but I can't let Baker take Riley, I can't. If it's the last fucking thing I do, I will save him.

Baker winces as the binding tightens around his body, squeezing. Snarling, he strains again. There's a sharp snap, and a crack forms down the center of the binding and in my chest.

"I told you," he pants out, "it's too late. You should be running, Burner."

The crack gapes wide before shattering open with the peal of a bell. That sound rips through me, digging into my chest like birdshot. A million sharp points of pain, caught within my rib cage and tearing through the soft organs within. Gasping, I fall to the ground, my vision going faint and gray-tinted at the edges.

Laughing, Baker shakes his arms out and flexes his fingers. "It was a good effort."

Before I can get to my feet, he hits me with a mass of power. I slam into the ground and slide across it, my shoulder aching and torn by the dirt and rocks. I push myself up on my arm, and I'm knocked back down again. Over and over, he pushes me into the dirt and soot, the flames licking around us held back only by the pressure waves of his blasts.

"It's funny, actually," he says as he walks through the burning field toward me. "I spent so long trying to get from the living world into Death that I never considered the power that would come from crossing the other way." He throws another wave of energy at me, and my ribs creak under the pressure. "Now, I have an unlimited conduit to Death and all of the power it brings. It's only a matter of time before I start gaining additional Affinities, and then"—his grin is like a death mask—"I will unlock the final Affinity and all of the strength it carries with it. No one will ever subjugate me again. Finally, I will be in control."

He looms over me. My mouth is full of grit and iron.

The toe of Cross's shoe is hard and unforgiving when it digs into my bruised ribs, Baker flipping me from my front to my back. He stares down at me, and all I see are Cross's eyes, flames reflected within.

"Cross," I gasp. "Riley, if you're in there, fight him. Please, you have to fight, if not for yourself, then for me. For us."

"Ah, young love," Baker sighs as he crouches down next to me. His hand snaps out to grip my throat. Choking, I grab at his wrist and fingers, trying to pull them away as he crushes my airway shut. "But people do love a tragedy, don't they? I will see you on the other side, Burner. If you see your grandmother, do tell her hello for me."

This is what Peterson warned me about. This is the end of the world, everything brought to its knees by Baker, by his impossibility. He died, he was Burnt, and he's returned with Death on his heels. I look up into Cross's face, desperate to find any sign of the man I love, but all I see is the end and alien eyes staring back at me with barely concealed glee.

Flames lick against the thin skin of my face. Baker's smile is skeletal. Everything is fading, black dots dancing in my vision as gray seeps in from the edges. My mouth opens and shuts as I desperately try to choke down even the slightest bit of oxygen. Bruised fingers fight for purchase. Baker's grip tightens, tightens. The pain begins to fade. Someone calls my name, their voice familiar and calming. They're waiting for me. Waiting for…

Purple light explodes around me in a wave, covering everything in twisting lines with a power I've never seen before. It's tightly coiled in Baker's eyes, in his chest, and some instinct makes me reach for it, even in my half-delirious, half-conscious state.

A tiny touch is all it takes, and my mind swirls, shifts, snaps.

When I blink, I stare down into my own vacant face, my blue lips parted in something close to a smile.

CHAPTER SIXTEEN

S omething alien brushes against my mind, and the brief moment of surprise is washed away by pain as that questing touch digs into me like claws.

No. The voice isn't one I recognize. It's deep and twisted like bones breaking, wet with chewed-up marrow. *No, you can't.*

Baker? Horrified, I pull away. But instead of my consciousness moving, Cross's hand—the hand that Baker controlled moments before, the hand I'm controlling now—lets go of my throat. My body crumples to the ground, my brain stem forcing a deep, gasping breath into my lungs. But though the color returns to my lips and cheeks, my eyes stay closed. There's nothing piloting my body, other than biological processes and mindlessly firing neurons.

My consciousness is somewhere else.

I stumble back as Cross's body moves in jerking, uncoordinated bursts. Unsteady and panicking as I grapple with what's happening, I pilot a body that feels unfamiliar, even though I know it intimately. It's different from the inside than the out, and though I know the sensation of Cross beneath my hands, the sense of him under my control is unsettling. Before I can regain my balance, though, there's a sharp pain in my head. Spinning away, I'm disconnected from Cross's body as quickly as I was connected to it.

I will not let you throw me out, Baker snarls in his blood-choked, broken-rock voice. *I have fought too hard for this.*

Well, tough shit, I Send, desperately fighting to orient myself. I'm trapped in a twilight world, and everything is spinning around me. There are brief moments of clarity as I slip into control of Cross's body, but then Baker throws me away, and I'm in darkness again.

Every time I grasp for control, Baker forces me away. His grip is like daggers in my mind. Flinching, I retreat, helpless. I'm still able to fall into Second-Sight, though, and that lets me see what's happening outside of Cross's mind.

The field in front of my parents' house is engulfed in flames. My body is, thankfully, in a patch that's more gravel than grass, and though the fire touches the edges of it, it doesn't come any closer. My breathing is easy and calm. It's almost like I'm sleeping.

Shocking how peaceful a coma can look.

When I try to shift back into my own body, nothing happens. There's a thin line of power connecting me to it, a purple thread as fine as silk. After I put my astral fingers to it, it hums like a power line or a guitar string, a low, rolling sound that's more feeling than noise. I wrap my hand around it and *pull*, and something shifts in my stomach like a landslide.

Oh, yes, Baker says, laughing. *Do that, Burner. Please,*

make things easier for me.

I immediately let go. *What is that?*

That, he says, smug and confident as he strides toward the house, Cross's long legs eating up the distance like it's nothing, *should be obvious.*

Hesitantly, I touch the line again. It hums through me. *It's me.*

Or it's another trick of mine. Go ahead, pull on it. See what happens when it breaks.

Convinced that the last thing I should do is anything Baker thinks is a good idea, I let go.

No matter how far we go from my body, the line stays taut between us. I'm reminded of the first time I met Baker, when he was possessing Richardson on the edge of Lake Michigan.

It's with a sickening dread that I realize it's the tie holding me to my body.

I curse. This is a whole different level of fucked. I have no idea how I ended up in Cross's body in the first place, and Baker's got literal decades of experience over me in how to use these powers. This isn't trying to figure out how to Read or how to Heal. I'm a fucking *Passenger* now, a Passenger who's possessing someone, and I'm fucking stuck.

Light swirls around me in Second-Sight, and I desperately cast about for my connection to Priya. It takes me a long time to find it, tangled as it is with the rest of the energy twisting around me, but it's there. Thin and faded to almost nothing, but still present.

I take hold of it with both hands and *pull*. Every part of my mind focuses on the task, and I desperately pour power into it, trying to strengthen the weak tie between us. It flickers, then brightens. Soon, it's glowing enough that it shows through my incorporeal grip, the memory of my bones backlit in my hand by the bond.

Kim.

Relief leaves me sagging, but I can't let go now. Instead, I focus all my energy and attention on our bond, almost insensate to what Baker is doing with Cross's body, where he's going, what his next move might be.

Priya, I need you, I Send, and only a moment later, she's back, floating next to Cross with confusion written across her face.

Her eyes glow white.

Oh, thank fuck. Priya, how the hell do I get out of here?

Out of... She blinks once, twice, and then her face stills. *Wait, Kim. Are you...?*

Yeah, but I don't want to be. I don't even know what happened, and now I'm just... Baker's too strong. I can't push him out, and I can't push myself out, and I don't know what to do.

Shaking her head, her black hair flying about in a nimbus, she reaches for me through the bond. *You need to get out of there.*

Yeah, I realize that, but how?

I don't know. Her touch is cold and slick as she touches my mind through the bond, but no matter how

many times she reaches out, I can't grab on. There's nothing to hold on to.

Baker pushes his way into the house, then starts tearing through drawers and cabinets, searching for something, though I don't know what.

Priya, frustrated, pulls away. *Can you Burn him from in there?*

Great idea, I say, *but I don't have any chalk or blood, or, you know, a* body. *I'm incorporeal, as far as I can tell.*

Can you feel him?

I watch as Baker breaks a vase that my dad bought for my mom on their seventeenth wedding anniversary. The porcelain snaps beneath his feet as he walks over the broken shards. As he moves, his motions echo in my mind. It's almost as if his actions are on a three-second delay. Even with the pause, I can feel him moving in whatever space we're occupying in Cross's mind.

Yeah, I think I can.

So, Priya says, as if it's obvious, *grab him.*

I don't bother responding, choosing instead to Send annoyance flickering through our bond.

Okay, fine, don't grab him. Let's look at this another way. How did you make the other Affinities work for you? she asks. *Just... How did you do it?*

You told me!

Baker's tread is heavy on the stairs as he hurries up them, glancing in and out of the bedrooms, still searching. I wrestle control of Cross's body from Baker for a moment and smell smoke. I take one step down the stairs—not knowing where Baker wants to go, but sure as hell not wanting to let him get there—before he rips me away and sends me spinning once again.

Nearly had him there.

Yeah, right.

Okay, what about Reading? Priya asks, clearly annoyed. *You figured that out on your own.*

I bled on something, and bam! I was Reading. I could try that again, but since I don't have a body *right now, I don't know how the hell I'm going to do that.*

He steps into my bedroom and lets out a happy sigh. "There we are."

Moving pointedly toward my duffel stuffed in the corner of the room, Baker kneels down and starts pulling clothes out. He quickly empties the bag and pauses.

On the Summoning and Capturing of Spirits sits, unassuming, in the bottom of the duffel.

Shit.

Baker's touch on the cover is almost loving. He draws the book out of the bag, dragging his hand over the cover before opening it. His fingers flip through the pages quickly before settling on the binding ritual.

"Finally," he sighs. I can sense his smile, though I can't see it. "After all this time."

Fuck. I've got to do something, and I've got to do it fast.

Reaching into the depths of my power, I pull energy

into the indistinct, liminal space I'm stuck in. My hands aren't really there, but I can feel my palms as they blister. Light slowly fills the space, all of Second-Sight subsumed by the blue-white glow.

Baker looks up, his hands stilling on the page.

"You think that will work?"

Pain lances through me. My head pounds. My hands ache. I pull more power.

"I already told you, Burner, it's over." He strokes the heading on the page. "It's all over."

I keep pulling power, keep dragging it into my hands and my body until everything aches and burns. My ears are ringing, and I want to shout, do anything to let this pain go.

Instead, I aim it all toward the edges of Baker that I can feel. There's a whump, like a fire suddenly extinguished, and Baker curses. That's cut off a moment later, too, and Cross's body falls face-first onto the bedroom floor.

Baker's on me a second later, his skeletal fingers digging into my psychic self like claws.

I'm going to enjoy killing you, Burner, he snarls, his breath dank and cadaverous in my face.

Pain lances through me. Though I don't have a body to rend apart, I can feel my skin and muscles tearing, can feel the snap of bones and the wrenching of tendons. The lights around me dim. The bond between me and Priya pulses in time with my racing heart.

Baker throws me away and steps back into Cross's

body. Groaning, he pushes himself to his feet, grabs the book, and hurries from the room. I'm still reeling as he reaches the first floor, as he bursts through the front door. There's fire everywhere, and he coughs as the smoke digs into his lungs.

I reach out for my bond with Priya, hand grasping as Baker heads to the car parked on the safe gravel drive. My touch lands on the purple thread to my body instead.

My connection to life.

I'll see you in Hell, asshole.

I wrap my fingers around the bond, and *pull.*

Chapter Seventeen

T he cord snaps, ringing through the empty space around me like a discordant bell. The longer the ringing goes, the more it shakes through me. My bones resonate with it, aching and off-key. A broken and wet voice screams.

What've you done? Baker's hands scrabble at mine, reaching for the thin purple line of power that lies limp in my grip. *You idiot child. You don't know what you've done.*

But as he fights to take that thread from my hand, I dig my fingers into his body. It's like pushing through rotten fruit. The flesh gives way, soft and yielding, but sickly hot. The putrescence of it gags me as I dig deeper, deeper, until I've got my fingers threaded through his ribs and feel the pulse of his heart against my fingertips.

Baker screams again, and his clawed hands turn frantic as they desperately try to break my grip on his body.

All the while, that off-key ringing grows and grows until it's all I can hear. A yawning void opens behind me, a blackness dotted with stars that draws me inexorably closer. Baker thrashes in my hand, and I finally have to let go of the broken thread to my body so I can twist my other hand around his bones. Flesh falls away the closer we get to the blackness, landing in great, steaming chunks on whatever intangible ground we're being dragged across.

No, he snarls. His fingers bite into my throat, my face, dig into the softness of my mouth and eyes. *You will not take me!*

I don't let go. Even as his thumb presses against my eye, deeper and deeper until I feel something burst, until hot liquid seeps over my cheek like tears, as I taste blood and foulness on my tongue.

If this is the end, I'm taking this bastard with me.

There's a moment of grief, a wash of emotion I only let myself feel for a breath. Riley's going to be furious with me, and heartbroken, maybe. And I never told him, never got up the courage to say…

The darkness draws me in and through. As I crest through the barrier, Baker's face comes into clarity before me. His sunken hollows of eyes and cheeks are split open and seeping. Blood drips over his face in sickening, black rivulets. It drips onto my face, coats my hands and arms, covers my chest as it pours from the wound I've ripped in his body. His fingers, more bone than flesh, are wrapped around my throat. With only my one working eye, he seems strangely two-dimensional, even though I can feel the solidity of his decaying body landing on top of mine as we hit the ground.

Behind his head, I see the hole we fell through. A familiar voice echoes through it, saying my name, but I can't remember who the person is or why they know me. All I feel is cool earth and hot blood and the thin prick of pain as my body lets go.

The creature on top of me is smiling. Its lips pull back from its teeth. Their points seem too sharp, the open wetness of its mouth too large as it grins. I wonder what I'll taste like when it devours me.

My fingers stay clenched around its ribs, drawing it closer even as it leans in.

Closing my eyes, I exhale.

The pain that lances through me isn't the pain of teeth in flesh. It's a lightning bolt of agony, a shaking, skittering feeling that rockets through me. It hits every nerve in my body, makes every muscle clench. Bones crack in my hands, and the creature roars. Its breath is rancid against my face, but all I can feel is pain.

Then *power.*

Endless, overwhelming, sweeping power. It fills me to overflowing. It pours from my mouth, my nose, my ruined eyes. It mixes with the blood and the decaying flesh, coats my body before it sinks back through my skin, filling me again and again until I'm lost in its swirling torment. All around me, power is black and red and glowing bright like flame. I'm burning up in it. My skin cracks. My flesh blackens.

I'm filled with color, with light. Blue-white. Red. Green. Yellow-gold. Orange. Pearl. Deep bruise purple. They twist and twine around me, dig into my broken body like razor wire knitting it back together. I'm a mess of light and dark, of solid strength and nothingness.

I give up. I give in. My hands fall from the creature's

chest as I fall back.

Everything stops.

There's no more pain, no more twisting uncertainty. All I feel is peace.

When I open my eyes, there's no more darkness.

I'm in a great open space. It's overcast, not bright but not the endless clouded sky it had been before. All around me are figures. Memories of humanity that have turned their misshapen and half-forgotten forms toward me. Their hands hang limp and heavy by their sides, though a few reach forward. Their voices are like the brush of wind through tall grass, a whisper of sound that builds and grows like a coming storm.

Keeper, they say. *The Keeper has come.*

Baker lies crumpled at my feet, his red-black eyes wide and terrified.

My body shifts and grows, until I'm towering over him and the rest of the creatures gathering around. Their shifting, crawling bodies remind me of insects, and I'm as capable of crushing them beneath my feet as if they were ants.

Baker shouts in rage, then rushes forward. His fingers in my leg feel like the pinprick of kitten claws, a distant tiny pain that's more nuisance than anything. I reach for him, my hand wrapping around his split-open chest with slow, ponderous movements. When my fist closes around him, he struggles against it, spitting and biting and clawing. It does nothing to stop the slow rise of my arm until I hold him before my ruined face, gazing down at him through my one eye.

They call me Keeper, I say. My voice sounds different in my mind. It's too deep, too distant. It's not my voice, not any longer, but something else entirely. It's power. It's wrong. *What is it I Keep?*

You keep nothing, Baker snarls. His hand swipes at my cheek, parting the flesh. Red and black flows over my skin, sizzling as it goes. I feel none of it, but when it hits Baker, he does. He thrashes and screams in my grip, and I watch with a detached disinterest that should feel wrong but doesn't.

What do I Keep? I ask again, directing the question to the growing crowd of souls around me.

Us, whispers the wind.

Discarding Baker feels like an afterthought. His broken body flies through the air and skids against the ground, but I barely notice it. As I bend down, my flesh shifts and flows until I'm small again and lost in the crowd of formless shapes around me. They run their misshapen hands over my body, each touch like a breath exhaled, like the softest of spring breezes. I reach out to them, and their fingers tangle with mine. They pull themselves closer and closer until our bodies meld.

I feel each one like a heartbeat in my chest, a swirling mass of warmth and pulsing life. More hands reach, and more bodies pour into me. Like the power before them, they fill me, but there's no pain, only peace, only surety that this is what I should be doing.

I am the Keeper. I will keep them safe, keep them warm, keep them whole.

Baker barrels into my back, throwing me to the

ground and scattering the crowd around me. The dark shapes fall back in the face of his anger, looking at me with formless mouths twisted in confusion and grief.

This isn't yours, he snarls. His hands tear at my body, ripping through my flesh and pulling souls free, casting them aside. *This isn't for you!*

An ember grows inside me as he takes more and more of what's mine. It feels familiar, feels like something I once knew. My bones shift and grow. There are claws at the ends of my hands now, and my teeth are knives in my mouth.

The Keeper has come, I growl. My body ripples, shifts. The memory of muscles and sinew grows. The ember burns brighter.

But not you. His hands wrap around my throat. His eyes are wide and wild, tainted with blood and desperation. *Not you*.

Flames burst to life within me, and I finally recognize the feeling for what it is. Anger, hot enough to blister. It courses through me like a forest fire, like the burning field before my parents' house. I've lost so much, given up so much, and now this fractured memory of a man is trying to take more.

I refuse to let him.

My claws rend the flesh from his shoulder in huge, gaping gouges. Blood pours from the wounds, black and coagulated, sluggishly running over his skin. It slicks my fingers, but does nothing to stop me from ripping more and more from his body. He screams, his hands loosening around my neck, and I twist my head to clamp my teeth over his wrist.

I taste decay, choke on it as his blood fills my mouth. When he twists again, trying to break free, his hand separates from his arm. I swallow it down, grinning with stained teeth as he screams again.

He keeps screaming until I press my teeth into his throat and cut off the sound with a crunch. Feeble hands push against my face, desperate and ineffectual, and I keep my mouth clamped tightly shut until they slow, like birds landing on water, before going still.

The limp weight of his body in my mouth is heavy. I let him fall to the ground. Eyes open and staring, I smile down at what remains.

The Keeper has come, I say before leaning down, mouth yawning wide and open.

I consume his body in one easy swallow, adding him to the collection of souls growing within me.

Us, whispers the grass.

They come closer. They press in. I reach out. Touch. Swallow. Devour.

The gray world turns red with blood, with flame. All around me, spots of light form. Brightness in the interminable ashen gloom draws me closer. When I put my hands into the light and pull, it grows larger and larger.

Bodies press against me. I draw them in.

The tear grows.

Kim!

I stop. The creatures gathered by my feet stop, turn

toward the voice.

Kim, you have to stop.

There's something familiar there. A pull deep in my gut, a thin string connecting me to something... someone.

You're breaking it apart, it says again. *You're going to bring it all down around us. You have to stop.*

There's a woman floating in the middle of the space. Her hair is a black halo around her face, her eyes bright white like the holes forming around me. They glow with power and with pain. Her face is streaked with tears, though her voice is soft and empty with sorrow.

I can't stop, I sigh. *The Keeper has come.*

And the Keeper can go. She draws closer, beseeching. *You're going to destroy everything if you don't.*

I look at the splintered sky, at the bloody ground, at the gathered souls all reaching for me, their mouths twisted in pain and grief. A great weight shifts in my chest.

I blink, my ruined eye aching.

Priya?

She collapses in on herself, the weight of her name crumpling her form with relief.

Oh, thank God. Are you back with me?

What's happening? I look at my arms, at the black talons growing from the ends of my fingers. Strange bony plates cover my arms and legs, and my stomach is bloated and distended. As I stare at it, uncomprehending, something shifts within it, a palm pressing against the skin, reaching out, before drawing back. *Oh, fuck, what's happening?*

I don't know, she says quietly. *But you have to fix it.*

I look away from my body, trying my best to ignore the way I can feel the things inside me moving. *How?*

You're the Keeper, she says, though I don't think she has any more of an idea what that means than I do. *Keep them with you.*

Gazing out across the empty plain, I see a black figure push its hand through one of the bright holes in the world, forcing its way through. It disappears, and that leaden instinct twists inside me again. Reaching for where the creature was a moment before, my arm extends longer than it can possibly go, my talons sliding through the hole with ease. Soil coats the tips as I touch the living world, but I pin the ghost, sight unseen, to the ground, and drag it back through.

It doesn't struggle as I pull it closer. Instead, it presses its body against mine, leaning into my skin, desperate and content to join the others.

I don't stop them from pushing into me. Instead, I call for them.

Let me hold you, I Send. *Stay with me.*

They turn from the tears, black eyes filled with reverence. They shamble and shuffle toward me. They fall into my body with remembered joy across their faces.

Power swirls within me, and I reach out with it gently. It's green and growing, and those vines of power twist and tangle their way through the tears, sealing them closed with bright, verdant energy.

Yes, Kim, Priya sighs. *You can do this.*

Bright blue-white light flows from me in waves, lapping gently against the legs and feet of the creatures that continue to gather. Flashes of red show me their pasts, their memories. Faces of loved ones, moments of joy, moments of sorrow. I cover them with gold, pressing comfort and ease into their minds. Pearlescent flashes of history and future, of what came before and what comes after, show me the final tear sealing shut, the red power seeping from a single symbol finally stymied.

A thin, purple thread cut by its closure.

Priya, I Send as the never-ending tide of creatures draws closer. *I'm sorry. He'll need you... when I'm gone.*

My hand wraps around her gently, talons turned back to blunt nails. I would never hurt her. I step closer to her, shrinking with each step, until my hand wrapped around her is resting on her cheek, and I'm staring into her swirling white eyes.

You won't be gone, she says softly, her smile inexpressibly fond. *I won't let you go. You're not the only one who wants to keep things, Kim.*

I can't leave them. I press a hand to my belly where I can feel the souls resting. They gather behind me, hands settling on my shoulders before they disappear into me. *They need me.*

They need a Keeper. It doesn't have to be you.

Vines twist around the broken hole in the sky, the one that Baker and I fell through an eternity ago.

Do you trust me, Kim? Priya asks, her hand tight around mine.

Of course.

Let it go. She pulls on our bond, her power coursing through it easy and sweet. *Let me take it.*

It starts as a trickle. A slow, almost unnoticeable slide of power from my body into hers. But as it grows, it speeds up until we're both awash in it. Her hand rests on my cheek, and mine rests on hers, and the energy swirling between us is a kaleidoscope of color and agony. It rips itself from me with gut-wrenching force, but Priya's hand on my skin gives me a point of focus, something to turn my attention to as I grit my teeth and wait for it all to end.

When it does, I feel empty… like a building burned through and left with charred timbers barely holding it up. Priya's hand on my cheek is the only thing keeping me on my feet, and as I stare up at her through my one good eye, she smiles, her eyes swirling with color.

I've always wanted to protect you, she says. Green seeps from her hand into my body, tangling its way through my veins and arteries and nerves. It soothes the aches, stitches it all back together. Healing washes, warm and confident, over me. When I blink, my eyelids heavy and slow, I can feel the sclera healing beneath, and when I open them again, I see her in vivid three dimensionality.

It's time for you to go back, Kim. She draws me close, wraps me in her too-large arms. When the power was in my body, I was twisted, misshapen. Priya glows with it. Her hair is lustrous and dark, shining as it cascades down her back to pool on the ground. Her body is strong and soft, powerful but yielding. She is a reed in the storm, thrown about but unbroken. A willow, her roots deep in the earth and unshakable, even as her branches dance with the breeze.

What about you? I ask, though I already know the answer.

Someone has to stay.

She lifts me to the quickly closing hole in the sky, growing with each second until I'm standing in the center of her palm. There's a hint of henna on her palms, and white lights are woven into her hair. She smiles, then leans forward to press her lips against my forehead. She could swallow me whole, could draw me into her body the same way she draws in souls.

Instead, she reaches through the tear with her too-large hand, and sets me into my body. As I gasp in a smoke-choked breath, my eyes burning, I reach for her desperately, fingers numb and heart aching.

Priya!

She smiles at me through the tear, her multicolored eyes wet. *I'll see you again, Kim. I love you.*

Priya!

And then she's gone.

CHAPTER EIGHTEEN

The tear slams shut.

"Priya!" My voice is rough, and as I yell her name again, I start coughing. I roll onto my front, gasping for breath, and look at the field. Everything is burning, and the flames creep closer to the house with every moment.

My fear for Priya disappears in a rush. All I can think about is Cross, unconscious somewhere nearby.

Aching muscles screaming as I force myself to my feet, I run through the flames. They lick at my clothes like ravenous creatures. I smell burning hair.

I don't stop.

I find his body sprawled out next to the car, left there when I dragged Baker into Death. Blood trickles from the corner of his mouth, and I can't tell if it's because he cut himself when he fell or if it's something more serious. I reach for Healing power, but find nothing. Whatever happened in Death, it sapped me of energy.

Cursing, I pat his pockets for the car keys and let out a relieved sigh when I find them. I unlock the passenger side door and wrench it open, then fight to get his heavy, unconscious body into the seat. Every instinct tells me to stop, to give up, but I push through the pain until Cross is half-slumped over the seat, his head resting on the center console, bleeding mouth parted.

"You fucker," I curse as I drag his legs into the car. "You asshole. If you fucking die on me, I swear to God, I will get you from Death and kill you again. Damn it, Riley, if you don't fucking wake the hell up and *help me...*"

I don't know when I started crying, but my vision blurs and I taste salt on my lips. His second leg is easier to force into the car. I pull him upright, drag the seatbelt across his chest and click it in. Secured against the seat, he slouches but stays upright, breathing easily.

There's a crash behind me, and as I turn, I watch one of the trees in the yard fall over, engulfed in flames. Burning branches and leaves scatter against the night sky like brilliant confetti, drifting toward the house. The first embers that land on the roof go out, but then flames lick at the shingles, their hunger unsated by the tree or the yard.

"Fuck." I fumble for my phone and curse again when I don't find it. "Fuck!"

We're out in the middle of nowhere. There's no way the fire department is going to get here in time to save the house. My memories of the place are the only thing of value left in its timbers, and those'll stay with me whether the house burns down or not. But there's a fallow cornfield in the property next to ours, and a farmhouse on the other side, and a family within.

I need a fucking phone.

I've done a lot of stupid things in my life, but running into a burning building to find a cell phone is probably at the top of the list. The roof isn't fully engulfed, and though I can hear flames crackling above me, I know I have at least a few minutes before it eats its way lower. My phone is resting on the nightstand, along with Cross's, and I grab them both before hurrying out of the room. There's no time to grab anything else, and there's nothing inside that means enough to me to try to save. Even the phones are more about trying to keep others safe, rather than any particular attachment I might have to plastic and glass.

Rushing through my parents' house for the open front door, I feel a strange disconnect from the world. It's almost like when Grandma Sadie dragged me out that night. It's the same sense of terror and relief, of shattered normality, only this time, my mom won't be watching from the porch, my father by her side. There won't be a guiding hand waiting for me after. No comfort to be found in someone else's surety.

I'll be alone.

I burst through the doorway and into the smoke-filled night, coughing. The flames on the roof have grown larger, and they're leaping from the eaves to the trees leaning over them. The sky is as bright as daylight, filled with twisting fire.

Jumping into the car, I slam the keys in the ignition, and tear down the drive, away from the engulfed remains of my parents' house. I stop by the road, hands shaking as I dial 911.

"McHenry County Emergency Dispatch." The woman's voice is pleasant, and my heartbeat slows with her calm confidence. "What's your emergency?"

"There's a fire." My voice cracks, and I fight against the urge to cough. "And it's spreading."

The firefighters are able to contain the blaze to my property. The house is a lost cause. Even if they arrived fast enough to stop the fire from gutting the place, the resulting water damage from the hoses is so bad that nothing would've been salvageable anyway. The field before the house is empty and barren, a blackened wasteland except for where the firefighters laid down a fire break to stop it from creeping onto the neighboring land.

I'm wrapped in a heavy-duty wool blanket pulled from one of the tanker trucks. They offered to take me to a local hospital, worried about shock, but I waved them off. I'm numbed through, still trying to process everything that's happened. Cross woke up a few minutes before the fire trucks arrived, eyes unfocused and voice slurred. At first, I worried he'd suffered a head injury from his fall, but as he dragged himself to sitting and wakefulness, the familiar intelligent spark in his eyes flared.

"Jesus," he said, looking over the burning field and house. "The hell did I miss?"

I laughed at first, but then it turned into gut-wrenching sobs, huge shaking things that made my tired body ache even more. Cross pulled me into his arms. Even though the center console dug into my side and the gearshift bit into my leg, I went with him, leaning against his body, dragging it closer, trying to hold on to something solid.

Hours later, he hasn't left my side. His hand rests in the center of my back, a delicate touch that's as much a comfort as his arms wrapped around me were. Even with his face streaked with blood and ash, he's stoic and steady.

The firefighters are nearly finished putting their gear away, and the tankers have already left, the hose trucks the only ones remaining. A few of the firefighters tip their hats to us as they wander past, but most give us space. They don't know us, but they recognize grief when they see it.

"So," Cross says as the last hose is rolled up and put away, as the final door slams shut and engines turn over. "Priya."

A knife twists in my gut. "Priya."

"She's gone."

I nod, unable to speak.

"She saved you?"

I turn into his body, pressing my forehead to his shoulder. My eyes ache. My cheeks are wet. He puts his hand on the back of my head, threading his fingers through my hair as I weep.

"I'm glad," he whispers into the newly darkened

night. "She loved you."

"I know."

"I love you."

I groan into his chest, my fingers tangling with his shirt. "You have the shittiest timing, Cross."

Laughing, he keeps running his fingers through my hair. "I know. Figured I should say it anyway."

We stand there for a long time, his arms wrapped around me as I slowly find my breath. The house creaks, its ruined frame shifting in a light wind. It'll all have to be torn down now. No more holding on to ghosts.

"We should go," he says into the cold night air. "There's no point in staying here."

Nodding against his chest, I pull back. He brushes his thumbs through the tear tracks on my cheeks, smiling fondly as I sniffle. After a quick kiss pressed to my forehead, he pulls away, leaving me cold without the warmth of his body against mine.

The drive back to the city is long and dark and quiet. The highway is relatively empty, but there's still a decent thread of traffic. People stay out of my way, though, lingering in the right-hand lane as I zip past in the left. Streetlights cut beams across the dashboard, flickering lines of light that beat out a soundless rhythm.

Cross doesn't say much from the passenger seat. His hand keeps migrating to his chest, rubbing the center of it almost mindlessly. I try to drop into Second-Sight, to see if there's still a gaping hole in the middle of him, but

I'm too tired, my energy too drained, to do anything more than fog my vision as I gaze through him. If he catches me looking, he doesn't say anything. His fingers brush my leg and drift back to his own.

I don't know why I drive us to his apartment instead of mine. I park and turn the car off. The engine ticks.

"You coming up?" he asks, and though he does his best to keep the surprise from his voice, I can hear it creeping in around the edges.

"If you'll have me."

"C'mon," he says as he unbuckles. "Let's go to bed."

When we get upstairs, I put my shoes by the door and the blanket from the tanker truck in a heap next to them. My clothes are stained with ash and smoke, and as I gaze at Cross's pristine, white apartment with growing horror, I'm immobilized by the sudden fear that I'll ruin everything I touch.

In an equally disgusting state, Cross kicks the door shut, toes off his shoes, and walks dirty and dusty and stained into the apartment. His fingers leave a black smudge on the door of the closet where his washer and dryer live. Stripping in the hall, he gives me a confused look, his dirty shirt over his head, his chest shockingly pale against the smudged, smoky darkness of his neck.

"You going to stay there all night?" He throws his shirt into the wash. "Or would you rather take a shower and get some sleep?"

I nod, numb, and wrestle out of my top. The sleeves tangle around my wrists, and Cross sighs before coming over to help free me. His touch is so gentle, I think I'm going to crumble like ash. His hands are stained when they come away, but he wipes them on my equally dirty shirt and throws it in with the rest of his clothes.

We finish stripping in the hallway. He starts the wash, then pushes me toward the bathroom. It doesn't take long for the water to get warm, and soon he's helping me into the shower, tilting my head back to wash the grime from it. It's so quiet, with only the sound of water and our breathing. We move back and forth, one of us standing under the spray while the other shivers at the far end of the stall. I wash my hair while he washes his neck and arms and hands. His chest, still scarred, looks so unassuming and normal without Second-Sight.

His head tipped back to rinse shampoo from it, I place my hand over the center of the symbol. He lets out a slow, gentle breath, then looks down at my palm pressed against his skin.

"I did this to you," I whisper, my fingers tracing the ridge of the scar. "I did all of this."

He presses my hand flat against his chest before stepping closer. I curl my fingers underneath his, staring at the way his thick fingers cover mine.

"Whatever you did," he says, "it's done. I don't know how I know, but I do. Something's different. I can feel it."

He's right. There's no pain where I touch him, no lightning-quick sting against my fingers. All I feel is warm skin and firm muscle and the gentle ridge where the Burner symbol is carved into his body.

He tilts my head back and kisses me. Water gathers between our mouths, but we ignore it, drinking each other down instead. It's slow and easy, both of us too tired to follow the low hum of desire between us. I reach behind him to turn off the water, and he passes me a towel when he steps out of the shower. Each wrapped in terry cloth, we go to his bedroom. My legs are still wet when I slide them between the sheets, but he doesn't say anything about the hint of dampness. Instead, he draws me into the shelter of his body, holds me close, and lets me fall asleep against him.

I try not to think of the echoing silence where Priya used to be.

I fail.

CHAPTER NINETEEN

W hen I wake up, Cross isn't in bed. There are quiet voices from the other room, too low for me to make out but enough of a noise to stop me from falling back asleep. I groan and roll out of bed, fumbling to get dressed. Every part of me hurts. My muscles are sore, and there are bruises all along my side from where I was thrown by Baker. The hair on my arms is singed away, and the skin is red and sore in places from where the flames got too close. Even my lungs ache, and each breath feels dust-choked. I finish pulling my shirt over my head, grab a couple of ibuprofen from Cross's bedside table, and swallow them dry. Hopefully, it'll be enough to take the edge off.

I rub the sleep from my eyes before stepping into the front room. Cross is sitting in the armchair, and across from him is Andrea. They look up when I walk into the room, their conversation cut off.

"Morning." I stand awkwardly in the hall while they turn to face me. "What's going on? Why're you here"

"The symbol." Cross presses his hand to his chest. "It stopped aching yesterday, after everything. Since Andrea's the resident expert, I gave her a call."

"From what Riley told me," Andrea says, "I'm surprised you're up already."

I fight back a yawn. "I thought I smelled coffee."

"It's still brewing." Cross shifts on the couch to make room for me, and I settle on the cushion next to him. It's warm from his body heat, though I still feel cold. His thigh presses against mine, and his smile is soft and steady.

"How'd you sleep?" he asks.

I shrug. "I slept."

Andrea looks at Cross, then back to me. Her expression is carefully twisted into patient expectancy. I'm not sure I like it.

She leans forward and laces her fingers together, elbows resting on her knees. "Do you want to talk about what happened yesterday?"

Not really. But if there's anything I've learned over the last couple of days, it's that sometimes I need to talk, even when I don't want to.

I laugh, and the sound of it is wild, even to my own ears. "I don't even know where to start."

"Well"—she glances at the door, then back to me— "I'm not going anywhere."

So, I try. It doesn't start easy, and I spend the first couple of minutes stumbling over my words, my lips and tongue failing to work together to form coherent sentences. Eventually, it comes pouring out of me like pus from a wound: the whole experience of sliding into Cross's mind and body, of falling into Death, the *power* and the way it warped my mind until Priya brought me back to myself.

And Priya. Her shining eyes, her light-dusted hair, and her smile, full of love as she pushed me back into Life, even though I was torn between wanting to stay with her and wanting to go.

By the end of it, Andrea doesn't look like she understands any more than she did before I started, but there's kindness in her eyes.

"I'm sorry you lost her," she says, ignoring my shaking hands as I wipe the tears from my face. "But I'm not surprised she did whatever she could to protect you."

"Well, she's gone now. Not much I can do about it." I fight back the grief.

Andrea laces her fingers together and stares at her hands. Then, looking up through her lashes at me, she asks, "Is that why you're Mundane?"

"What?"

"Kim." She leans forward. "You must have noticed."

I try to drop into Second-Sight again, but the room goes blurry and distant instead. I refocus on Andrea, on her sympathetic eyes, on the certainty in her voice.

"I didn't…"

"Just…" Andrea pushes her hair back. "Close your eyes and listen to my voice."

"Why?"

"Because, you brat, I'm trying to help you."

I sigh and close my eyes. Sitting in the darkness, I take slow, even breaths.

"I want you to picture you're somewhere safe, somewhere that makes you feel happy. Whatever that looks like, I want you to imagine it as clearly as possible. Nothing can hurt you there. Nothing can touch you. There's no pain, no worry. All you feel is calm and peace. Settle into that feeling. Let it hold you."

As my breathing steadies and I fall into her voice, the pain—physical and emotional—fades. All that's left is the steady push and pull of my blood moving through my body, the low pulse of my heartbeat, the in and out of air in my lungs. It's dark and quiet. Easy.

"Wherever you go, that peace will go with you. You are safe."

The words fall from my mouth like forgotten things lost. "I am safe."

"Good. I want you to get up from wherever you are. I need you to search for something. It's part of you, but it's not easy to find. You can feel it drawing you toward it. Follow that feeling, and when you find it, tell me."

Though I don't move, I stand. I walk through the dark, quiet world. Each step feels like trudging through heavy snow. Reality clings to my feet and legs, slowing me down. But there's no pain, no fear. I keep moving forward, sluggish step by sluggish step. On the horizon, there's a muted sun rising.

"I see it," I say as I try to hurry forward. The ground grabs me, holds my feet tight. I pull one foot free, then the other. "I see it."

"What does it look like?"

There's a low red light, like the embers of a great fire left to gutter out overnight. The heat of it stings but also soothes. I want to put my hand into it, to hold the warmth of it close, but I'm buried up to my knees in the ground, and I can't move any closer.

"It's nearly gone." My voice is choked with tears. "It's fading."

She sounds hopeful, but so distant. "But it's still there?"

"Yes." I reach for it, unable to touch. "Yes, it's still there."

"Good," she sighs. "That's good. Now come back, Kim."

"I don't... I can't."

"You *can*." Another voice, this one deeper. It pulls at me like gravity, an inescapable force that I don't want to escape. "Come back."

My legs scream, but I force myself to turn, to rip my feet from the ground, to scrabble and tear at the black until I creep forward, inch by inch. It gets easier the farther away from the embers I go, but the cold creeps in with each step, and I turn back to stare at the low, red glow on the horizon, again and again, until I can't see it anymore.

When I open my eyes, Cross holds my hand in his. He squeezes gently, his smile soft and sad. "Welcome back."

My voice is scratchy when I speak. "What was that?"

"That," Andrea says softly, "is your power."

"But it's…" My tongue is thick and stupid. "It's gone."

She nods, and the room falls silent. Cross laces his fingers with mine.

"I'm sorry." He places his other hand of ours, as if he's holding me together. "I'm so sorry, Kim."

I shake my head. There's a ringing in my ears that I can't stop. Whatever he says next, I don't hear it. All I can do is stare into the middle distance, trying to find Second-Sight and failing, over and over again.

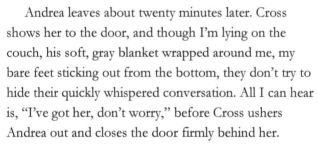

Andrea leaves about twenty minutes later. Cross shows her to the door, and though I'm lying on the couch, his soft, gray blanket wrapped around me, my bare feet sticking out from the bottom, they don't try to hide their quickly whispered conversation. All I can hear is, "I've got her, don't worry," before Cross ushers Andrea out and closes the door firmly behind her.

He gives me a long look, then nods before wandering into the kitchen. A minute later, he comes back with a glass of water. Ice floats at the top, and condensation is already forming on the glass when he puts it in my hand. It sticks to my fingers, and when I take a sip, the ice hits my teeth.

"I'm going to make something to eat," he says when I set the glass down. "You want me to bring you a plate?"

"Sure, if you want." I pull the blanket closer. "I'm

not hungry."

"I'll make you something light, then. Peanut butter and jelly okay?"

I nod, and he heads back to the kitchen. My mind drifts while he's gone. I keep reaching for my power, for Priya, and have to fight the urge to shiver when neither respond.

Everything feels *wrong*. It's like I've lost an arm, though I can still feel the way the muscles flex and tighten. I reach with a hand that isn't there, surprised when I come back with nothing in my grasp.

I've been Sighted since I was a kid. I don't know what it's like to *not* be able to see ghosts or the energy flowing through the world. Somehow knowing it's there but being unable to feel it is the worst part. Sudden sympathy for Andrea wells within me, and I gather the blanket between my fists for something to hold on to.

Some of my distress must be visible on my face, because when Cross comes back into the living room with two sandwiches balanced easily on plates, he blanches and hurries over.

"Hey, hey, it's okay," he says, falling to the ground next to the couch and grabbing my hands between his. "It's all right, Kim. I'm right here."

The sobs catch me off guard, but then I'm crying again. Grief bowls me over, and Cross is there to catch me. I press my face into his shirt and block out the light. It's easier in the dark.

He eases me to the side until he can sit on the couch with me, and I curl into his body, my hand still clenched in his shirt. Whispering quiet nothings into my hair, he rubs my back and I shake apart.

It's a long time before my sobs quiet and settle, and by the time they do, I'm wrung out and exhausted. Cross still has his mouth pressed to the top of my head. Without the background of my crying, I can just make out what he's been saying.

"I know she loved you, but I love you, too. You aren't alone. I'm right here."

Over and over, he says it. Softly, like saying it too loud will cause the words to crack and fall away. His arms are pressed around me, his lips pressed to my head, his love pressed against every inch of my breaking heart.

"Cross." My voice is rough and clogged with tears. I pull back until he meets my eyes. "Riley."

He smiles, then kisses me as soft as a breeze. Pushing my hair behind my ear, he cradles my face and rubs at the tear tracks until they dry. I turn my head into the caress and let my mouth rest against his palm. It's barely a hint of a kiss.

"You're gonna get through this, okay? I know it seems hard, but I've never seen you back down from a challenge."

"I need to… You have to know."

His body tenses beneath my hands.

"Please don't tell me you've been keeping more secrets, Kim. I don't think I can handle any more right now."

I laugh, and it comes out like a sob against his palm. "Just one more," I say. "And it's the last one, I promise. Probably."

He starts to pull away with a sigh, and I grab his wrist, keeping his hand against my face. Disappointment hangs heavy around him, but he doesn't try to pull away.

I don't deserve him or his patience.

"Just tell me," he says with another sigh. "Let's get this fight over with."

"I love you."

He freezes, and I laugh again. Pressing a kiss—a real one—against his palm, I curl his fingers around mine so I can kiss his knuckles and his broad, competent hands.

"You what?"

Mouth pressed against his skin, I say it again. "I love you."

"Well." He's smiling. "So much for the fight."

I don't know who moves first, but we fall against each other in a rush. My arms wrap around his chest, and his wrap around my back, one hand cradling the back of my head as I bury my face into his neck. His laughter tickles my ear, and for a moment, I'm able to forget the grief, the pain, the uncertainty.

Wrapped up in each other, the world falls away and, at least for now, I'm happy.

CHAPTER TWENTY

D istrict headquarters is quiet in the early morning. The night shift is finishing up, but the morning crew hasn't arrived yet. Riley and I pull into a parking spot near the front and climb out. My detective's badge hangs around my neck, and the weight of it against my chest is both familiar and uncomfortable after not wearing it for the last two weeks. It thumps against my shirt with each step, and the tempo drives me through the doors and toward Lieutenant Walker's office.

Her head is tipped down, her desk covered in neat piles of paperwork. When we enter, she looks up and gestures for us to close the door.

"I need a minute. Go ahead and sit, and then we'll get into it."

Riley nods, letting me take a seat first. I want to roll my eyes at the small show of chivalry, but as far as I can tell, it's more Riley being polite than anything else.

"Okay." Walker closes a manila folder and pushes it to the side. "There, that's done. Thank you for being patient. Now, tell me. How are you two doing?"

"Fine, ma'am," Riley says. "I believe we're both

ready to return to the field."

"That's good, that's good. Phillips? Do you agree?"

I nod. "Yes, ma'am."

"Because you look like dog shit."

"Thank you, ma'am."

She glares at me. "I mean it. Are you sure you're fully recovered? Concussions can be difficult."

"It's not the concussion." I take a breath before I add, "My parents' house burned down two nights ago."

"I'm sorry to hear that. Was anyone hurt?"

"No, no one was injured. Just property damage."

She leans back in her chair. "That's a relief, though I'm sorry about the house. But if you're both otherwise recovered, then I think we can start talking about next steps."

"Is it not as simple as taking us off leave?" Riley's expression is carefully neutral, but I can hear the annoyance in the edge of his voice.

"Yes, and no." Walker shifts through the papers on her desk and pulls out another folder. The CONFIDENTIAL stamp across the front makes me pause. "IAB has some questions for you, and while that's the case, you're both prohibited from doing any field work."

"You're putting us on desk duty?" I look at the case file, then back to her. "For how long?"

"I don't know. That's entirely dependent on how long the internal investigation goes on."

"How long it…" I push the anger down, fighting to

hold it in. "With all due respect, Lieutenant, there's no way the investigation won't take a significant amount of time. Considering the extent of what we saw from Cooper's activities alone, this could last years."

"Yes, I am aware of that possibility."

"You have to be kidding me." Riley's pale, his mouth open with surprise. "Detective Phillips and I weren't involved in whatever Cooper was getting up to."

"I know that, and you know that, but IAB is under a lot of pressure to keep everything aboveboard. The optics on this aren't—"

"The optics? We're talking about optics right now?"

Walker places her hand on top of the folder, and though she does it without a shred of anger, the motion makes me stop talking.

"You have both been high-profile members of the force for the last year. You've investigated multiple homicides that drew significant media attention. You were just in a goddamned building collapse, one that ended with a Turned ghost and a Chicago police detective shooting lasers from his hands and passing out while on camera." She smiles tightly. "So, yes, we are talking optics right now."

"I didn't become a cop to sit behind a bench and fill out paperwork for who knows how long."

"That's part of the job, Phillips. Better get used to it."

Nausea twists in my gut. As I stare at her and her

vast desk full of folders, the tidy piles in her in and out bins, the boxes on the counter behind her desk, I swear I'm Seeing into my own, horrific future.

"I won't do it."

Her eyebrows shoot up, nearly disappearing into her hairline. "You what?"

"I'm not pushing papers for the rest of my career."

"It won't be the rest of your career, Phillips," she snaps.

"No, it won't."

My hand is shaking as I lift my badge from my chest and pull it over my head. The chain is warm when it hits my hand, but the silver star is cold. I set it on her desk.

No one speaks.

Riley turns in his chair, eyes wide. "What are you doing?"

"I'm quitting." My ears are ringing. "I quit."

"Detective, I—"

Before Walker can say anything else, I shove my chair back and get to my feet. Numb, I walk to her office door, open it for the last time, and hurry into the bullpen. A few heads lift as I exit, but I'm too focused on the double doors to the parking lot to note who's shown up for work and who's left.

I push my way outside and head straight for my car. I hear the doors slam open behind me as I fumble for my keys.

"Kim!" Riley grabs my arm, stopping me from unlocking my door. "What the hell was that?"

I wrench my arm from his grasp and drop my keys in the process. Cursing, I kneel down, but he's right there with me. My hand slaps down over the keys, his hand landing on top of mine and holding it against the pavement. For a moment, I consider wrenching my hand out from under his, but when I look up, his expression is soft, expectant.

"C'mon. Talk to me."

He squeezes my hand gently and waits. I want to look away, but I can't.

"I can't do it."

"Desk duty won't last forever," he says with a smile. "Walker says it's indefinite, but we both know she'll cave after a few months."

"No." Frustrated tears prickle at the corners of my eyes, and I hate that everything seems to make me cry these days. "I can't be a cop anymore."

His hand spasms against mine. "What?"

"When I was a kid and seeing ghosts, the ones who died violently always talked about punishment, about finding the person who killed them and bringing them to justice. I always thought that I'd be a better cop because I could see them and talk to them. I could bring them justice when no one else could."

I drag in a ragged breath and go on. "So, I became a cop because I was a Medium. And now… I'm not a Medium anymore, Riley. It's gone. And I don't know if I can be the kind of cop I want to be without it."

"You're a great cop, Kim. You don't need powers to

do this job or to do it well."

I sigh, then turn my hand up underneath his so that the keys are cupped between them and our fingers interlace. "I know that. But I also don't think I want to *be* a cop if I'm not a Medium. I've spent so much of my life around death, and I can't help but wonder what it'd be like if I just… didn't anymore."

"It still seems rash. I didn't know you were even considering it."

"I've spent so much of my life worrying about others, taking care of others. And now, a huge part of how I did that is gone, and I… I don't know, I want to try living for *me* for a while."

"And it's not because of everything that's happened over the last couple of days? Because you lost…"

"I think she'd want me to be happy," I say, though it hurts. "I think she'd want me to be free. I don't think I can do that and stay a cop."

"Okay." He squeezes my hand. "If you're sure. I think Walker would let you walk it back, turn it into a leave of absence if you wanted."

I shake my head. "No, it needs to be final. If I keep it in some half state, I'll never move on. It'll be too easy to stay."

"And you're not going to regret it in a few days? A few weeks?"

"No, I don't think so." There's so much uncertainty, but the more I think about it, the more sure I feel. "It's the right choice."

"So," he says, drawing out the syllable, "what's next?"

"I've got my parents' house to consider. I can't just leave it the way it is, and with the insurance money, it might make sense to rebuild and sell the place. Who knows, maybe I'll move out of the city."

"Hey, now," he says with a smile, "let's not get wild."

"You, uh… You're welcome to join me, if you want. I mean, I'm not asking you to quit, that's your decision to make, but if you want to come help with the house when you've got the time…"

"Of course I'll help you." He squeezes my hand. "C'mon, Kim. I'm not going to abandon you because we don't work together anymore."

"That's my bad," I say, holding back a smile. "I assumed you were only with me so I'd do your share of the paperwork."

"Trust me, that's never been a motivating factor for me." He squeezes my hand one more time and gets to his feet. "I need to go back in there. I kind of rushed out after you without much of an explanation, and I'm sure the Lieutenant has questions."

"I guess I'll see you later?"

"Yeah, I'll head over to your place once I'm done here."

"See you then." I nod toward the doors. "Good luck in there."

"I'm going to need it."

We smile at each other for a moment, neither of us ready to let the other go. Riley shakes himself out of it and heads back to the door. A moment later, cursing, he runs back, captures my face in his hands, and kisses me. I sink into it, letting it soothe my rough edges. It's good and warm, and with each brush and press of his lips against mine, a bit more of my uncertainty slips away.

This, at least, is steady, strong.

"Okay, now I really have to go," he says against my mouth. With a final, soft kiss, he pulls away. He tucks my hair behind my ear, smiles, and goes back inside.

I watch him disappear into the building. Outside, the sun is warm against my face.

I smile.

Epilogue

Two Months Later

Hands on my hips, I lean back and sigh as my spine cracks. I wipe the sweat from my forehead and grimace at the gritty streak my work glove leaves behind.

The dumpster is full of charred wood. After the place was bulldozed, there was a massive pile of what remained. I've been chipping away at it, bit by bit, while the construction crew got the new frame up. Built on top of the existing foundation, the wooden framing looks like new growth creeping its way from the earth. Even the smell of ash and charcoal is covered by the omnipresent scent of wood chips and cut lumber. It smells good.

My back twinges as I stop stretching, and for a moment, I let myself miss being able to move things with my mind. I was only a Shaker for a short amount of time, but right now, I wish I could reach out and move things without having to strain any of my muscles to do it.

I find myself dropping into Second-Sight at the

oddest moments, though I fail to see anything other than a blurry approximation of the world. There are no lines of power, no blue-white light infusing everything around me. Just the living, breathing world in all its simple, complicated glory.

Though I try not to, I miss it.

I don't miss being on the force, though. In some ways, it's easier without it. I've fallen back on some of my savings, some of the money Grandma Sadie left me when she passed, some of the insurance money from my parents' house. It's enough to get by, and Riley is helping where he can. And since I don't need the cash, it's easier to let the rest of it go.

It's not so easy to let Priya go, though. I keep looking for her, waiting for her voice in my mind and her cool touch on my shoulder. When I wake up and my brain is still fuzzy with sleep, I swear I can feel her with me, waiting, watching.

Of course, she's never there.

With nothing better to do than wait for the remains of my parents' house to get torn down, I lost myself in the stacks at the Newberry. I was there often enough that I managed to learn the reference librarians' names and shifts, and they knew to have a handful of the more esoteric books set aside for me when I arrived.

There hadn't been anything about Keepers, and trust me, I looked. Nothing about an eighth Affinity or some great power in Death that held it all together and in check. The only thing I found that hinted at something similar was a collection of children's rhymes from the

1700s, and even that was only if you squinted at it. Whatever I became in Death—that Priya still was— wasn't anything that had been written about before, though I wondered what I would find if I could manage to get my hands on Baker's research materials.

I miss Priya constantly. My chest aches with it, and I struggle to not dwell on the pain, like poking at a bruise until it stings. Instead, I like to think of her caring for the souls in Death. She always was a caretaker, and I imagine she's taken to nurturing the dead as easily as she took to nurturing me.

Losing her, as much as it hurts, seems to have been worth the cost, though. Andrea has been keeping in touch, letting me know what's going on with the supernatural world I can no longer see. The red-black energy is fading all across Chicago, and the markers seem to be disappearing, too.

"Dave's gone," she told me one early Sunday morning over coffee and breakfast sandwiches. "And so is the energy he was guarding. It's like they were never there. Even the inscriptions on the marker are missing, and I have no idea how they managed to do that. I mean, they were carved into the stone. It's not like they could fill them back in, not without making it obvious."

But I think about how I was able to tear down an entire building with my power, and how Peterson's contacts in the Medium community likely span the nation, and part of me believes her group could find a Shaker talented enough to pull the rock up from inside a rune and make it all smooth again.

On top of that, the morning's *Trib* had an article about a rising cry from social media to tear down the Confederate Memorial at Oak Woods. It's too close to Dave's disappearance to be a coincidence. I wonder if Peterson has anything to do with it, though it's one of those things I'll never be able to prove.

I'm not sure I care to.

The energy seeping from Riley is gone. No more hole to another plane of existence in his chest, no more caustic power eating away at him, just the slightly raised scar emblazoned across his chest, and even that is fading. The scar isn't quite so pink, and sometimes I forget it's there when I run my hand over his skin. He still rubs at it, though I think that's more from habit than from pain.

While I'm working on rebuilding my parents' house, Riley is still working for the CPD. Thankfully, his foray into desk duty has ended up being less of a punishment and more of a relief for him. For some godforsaken reason, he seems to enjoy shuffling papers around and working his way through cold cases. He's found a handful that look promising, and he's planning on asking Walker for permission to reopen them once IAB's done with him. Cooper's ring of dirty cops is bigger than anyone expected, though, so there isn't much hope Riley will be let back into the field any time soon.

It's odd being on this side of things when it comes to the police. I'm disconnected from it in a way I haven't been since before I went into the academy.

Looking from the outside in, I notice the cracks more. I was able to ignore it when I was neck-deep in things, but now… Well, let's just say that I haven't regretted my decision to leave the force.

Riley and I don't really talk shop. Sometimes, when he comes home from work, exhausted and heartsick over something he's read about or overheard in the bullpen, he'll talk to me about it. But for the most part, he keeps the police stuff to himself and focuses instead on our relationship and what it looks like to be a couple without being partners.

From my view, it looks pretty good.

The sun is setting, and as I crack my back one more time, I let the weary ache in my muscles settle something in my soul. It feels good to be tired and sore from a hard day's work with my hands. It's simple, satisfying. The dying light cuts through the skeletal frame of the house and casts long shadows on the grass. It's already growing back from where it burned, the shoots healthy and green among all of the soot.

There's probably something poetic about it, though I don't have the words to describe it. Looking at all the new green, though, makes me smile.

Life goes on.

I climb into the car as the sun finally dips below the horizon. When I point my wheels back toward downtown, the darkening sky glints with the faint lights of the city. Their blue-white shine draws me closer, draws me home. Street lights flash their way across my dash, and I hurry east, back into Chicago and the towering skyscrapers and crushing humanity. It feels good.

I feel good.

Blue-white flickers at the edge of my vision, and I glance out of the corner of my eye to trace the thin line of light along the highway. There's something familiar about it, but it's gone as soon as I look at it fully.

There's probably an explanation for the glow, but I decide to worry about that later.

Some mysteries don't need to be solved.

GLOSSARY OF TERMS

Medium — A person possessing the ability to interact and communicate with the afterlife and spirits of deceased people. Mediums make up about 0.2 percent of the population, depending on the area. They Bond with ghosts who have yet to Turn as the final step of their training, which increases their power and stops the ghost from Turning.

Turning — When a ghost loses their sense of reality and becomes dangerous to living people. After Turning, ghosts may cause damage to property, as well as people.

Affinity — The specialized skill set a Medium possesses. The seven Affinities, from most common to least, are Burner, Reader, Healer, Speaker, Shaker, Seer, Passenger.

Burner — This is the most common type of Medium. They can speak with and exorcise ghosts and usually work in criminal justice or as independent contractors.

Reader — Gains memories and emotions from physical objects. Clarity of images and depth of information is dependent on their power and how long they're in contact with the item. The longer they spend trying to find out information from something, the better it is, but there is a limit to what they can discover. Most items will not trigger anything when a Reader is in contact with them, but some items that have a strong psychic aura will cause them to fall into a vision without warning. Second most common type of Medium.

Healer — Possesses healing abilities and can view internal structures. They are regarded with extreme respect and sought out regularly by hospitals and convalescent homes. They tend to be very caring individuals, who form significant emotional bonds with the people they trust and love. The strength of the Medium determines how severe of an injury or illness they can heal. Third most common type.

Speaker — Can communicate telepathically with other Mediums and people who have a predisposition for the supernatural. Work with Burners and Readers regularly. Also tend to work in special forces or the military due to their ability to Speak to people. The strength of the Medium determines how far and how many people they can Speak with at a time. Fourth most common type.

Shaker — Can move things and people without physically touching them. The weight of the item or person they can move is determined by the Medium's power. They tend to work in dangerous construction jobs, like underwater drilling and high-rise construction and repair. They are also commonly found working in disaster areas, especially earthquakes, as support teams. Fifth most common type

Seer — Can see into the future or past. The length of time into the future or past and the clarity of what they See is based on their inherent power. Generally work in the financial, military, or political sector. Sixth most common type.

Passenger — Can possess people for brief moments. Very little is known about this Affinity as it is so uncommon. They have been steadily declining in numbers since the early 1800s. Almost no Mediums of this type are alive currently. Seventh most common type.

Second-Sight — The specialized vision that Mediums use to view and interact with elements of the afterlife. Said to appear as a brightly lit outline of the living world.

Sending — When a Medium or ghost shares a memory or thought with another Medium or ghost. Used as a form of communication for Mediums and their partner ghosts, as well as Speakers when communicating with other Mediums.

Circle — A circle written in chalk used by Mediums to do various things, such as Burning a ghost or Seeing something that happened previously in a location. The function is determined by the sigils and runes used to construct the circle. Powered by the blood of a Medium, otherwise inactive. Will completely disappear after being used.

Runes — Arcane marks that describe the nature of things. Used in circles to describe what the circle is supposed to effect.

Sigils — Arcane marks that link runes together and focus arcane energy in circles. Directs and channels energy in circles.

Wards — Sets of sigils and runes used outside of a circle to protect an area from entry or exit. Generally used on Mediums' homes to stop malevolent or unknown ghosts from entering. Can also be used to stop a ghost from leaving an area.

ACKNOWLEDGEMENTS

I really don't know how to start this acknowledgement. This is usually my favorite part of finishing one of these books, but it feels wildly different this time, knowing that I won't be coming back to Kim and Riley in a few months.

This isn't the book I thought it was going to be. Eagle-eyed readers might notice that, for one, the title is different. When I finished Speaker, my plan was to continue writing one book per Affinity, closing the series with Passenger. But as I sat down to plot out the next book, I found myself struggling to find a story that I could make work across three more novels.

After a lot of talking (and worrying and stressing and then talking again) with my husband and other writer friends, I made the decision to end the series earlier than I originally planned. I just didn't have enough gas in the tank to get another three books written, as much as it pains me to admit it.

Now, all of that being said, this is still how the story was going to end. We just got to it a bit faster. I'm happy with the ending, even with the little bit of openness in the epilogue. I like that it gives me the flexibility to come back to this world if I so choose. I know you all love it as much as I do, and I'd hate to say goodbye forever.

It does leave me with a bit of a question, though: What's next?

I'm still figuring that out, though I feel like I have a million ideas for a new world, new characters, new stories. I hope you'll want to come along for that ride with me, the same way you stuck through the Affinity Series with me. I can't wait to see what the future brings.

I want to extend my thanks, again, to the Indianapolis Police Department members who assisted me throughout the series. Though many of them are no longer with the IMPD, their knowledge of police work and procedure was invaluable over the last almost-decade. Thank you, Officers Nick Gallico, Frank Miller, and Michael O'Conner.

Big thanks to my writer friends, Bella and Ola. You both pushed me when I was losing steam on this story, and I don't know if I could've done it without your cheerleading and encouragement. I adore the both of you, as you well know.

I've said it in every acknowledgement in the series, but my editor, Nikki Busch, is a godsend. Working with you has been such a pleasure, and I can see how much I've grown as a writer with your guidance and help over the years.

My husband's constant, unyielding support as I've worked on this series has proven, repeatedly, that I was absolutely a genius to have married him. Thank you, my love, for all your patience, encouragement, and not-so-gentle suggestions to hide from the kids so I could write. I don't know what I'd do without you.

And finally, to my readers. I don't know how to tell you all how much you mean to me. That anyone would be willing to take a risk on my stories and characters still staggers me, and to know so many of you have stuck with Affinity since day one is more humbling than I can express. Thank you for your trust and your support. Thank you for loving these characters as much as I do. And thank you for being so patient as I've finished the series. I hope I did all of you justice with this ending.

I'm still deciding if I'm going to take a break from writing or not. Like I said above, I have plenty of ideas, but I'm still figuring out the next steps in my writing career. If you want to stay in touch or see how I'm doing (or what I'm working on), you can always follow me on Twitter (@p1013). I love hearing from you, even if it's just to say hi.

Thank you all so much. I really, really, couldn't have done this without you.

ABOUT THE AUTHOR

J. S. Lenore was born and raised in the suburbs of Chicago. She attended Elgin High School, graduating within the top ten of her class. She majored in Japanese Studies at Earlham College and graduated with honors before getting her Masters in Teaching, also from Earlham College. She started creative writing at a young age, mainly writing fanfiction, but did not find much success until after graduation. In 2013, writing under the handle p1013, J. S. Lenore posted her first fanfiction for MTV's *Teen Wolf.* This story, titled *The Full Moon Like Blood*, and others gained a moderate following. In the same year, she decided to branch out into original fiction, writing the rough draft of *Burner* during National Novel Writing Month. She's since written five novels in the Affinity Series.

J. S. Lenore currently lives in Indianapolis with her husband, two children, one cat, one dog, and zero ghosts.